T0035890

"[Armfield's] insights into the grieving process sometimes stop you in your tracks. . . . Moving and evocative . . . Kept me turning the pages. Armfield has a deep feel for language. . . . The final scene in Miri's narrative absolutely floored me. . . . It moves me to tears just thinking about it now."
—*Washington Independent Review of Books*

"[A] masterpiece . . . Deeply romantic and devastating."
—*Refinery29*

"Without a doubt, *Our Wives Under the Sea* is one of the best books I've ever read. It's not only art, it's a perfect miracle. We are lucky for it."
—Kristen Arnett, author of
With Teeth and *Mostly Dead Things*

"A wonderful novel, deeply romantic and fabulously strange. I loved this book."
—Sarah Waters, author of *Tipping the Velvet*

"I was entirely captivated by this book. A gorgeous debut."
—Jami Attenberg, author of *I Came All This Way to
Meet You* and *The Middlesteins*

"Beautiful, otherworldly, like floating through water with your eyes open."
—Daisy Johnson, author of *Sisters* and *Everything Under*

"Julia Armfield is one of my favorite writers. *Our Wives Under the Sea* is a contemporary gothic fairy tale, sublime in its creepiness."
—Florence Welch, lead singer of Florence and the Machine

Praise for *Our Wives Under the Sea*

A Best Book of the Year (NPR, *The Washington Post*,
Literary Hub, Goodreads, Tor.com, *them*, and more)
Long-listed for the Carnegie Medal for Excellence in Fiction
A Goodreads Choice Award Finalist

"Shocking . . . Achingly poetic . . . Sharp and beautiful as coral
polyps . . . Armfield exercises an exquisite—even sadistic—
sense of suspense. She's cleverly designed this story so that we
only gradually become aware of how little we know. 'Panic
is a misuse of oxygen,' Leah warns, but by the climax of this
eerie novel, I was misusing it with abandon."

—Ron Charles, *The Washington Post*

"A deeply strange and haunting novel in the best possible
way . . . An impressive and exciting debut novel that may leave
you thinking about your own relationships in a new light."

—NPR (A Best Book of the Year)

"A haunting, evocative novel that juxtaposes the horrors beneath
the waves with the life and love that exist on land."   —*Time*

"Armfield uses this mysterious setup to explore anticipatory
grief and the limits of human understanding, and I was a little changed after reading *Our Wives Under the Sea*, too."

—*The New York Times*

"Sublimely gorgeous . . . Readers are treated to a stunning love
story about a couple trying to make sense of their new unfamiliar situation, while also learning about what happened
to Leah on the ocean floor. It's pretty much perfect."

—Liberty Hardy, *Book Riot*

"Hypnotic . . . Gripped me from the first chapter . . . Armfield is unafraid to deal with uncomfortable issues, asking readers how much it's possible to ever really know someone, no matter how long you've been with them. I savored each delicious sentence of *Our Wives Under the Sea*, underlining passages on almost every page, and genuinely missed the characters when it ended."
—*BuzzFeed*

"Armfield has written a novel so chock-full of stunning sentences that that urge to scream needled its way into me throughout my first *and* second reads of the book. . . . It isn't an obvious monster novel, but I consider it a monster novel in its own way. A deeply queer one, a deeply romantic one."
—*Autostraddle*

"Original and haunting."
—*People* (Best New Books)

"If you're in the mood to cry, then Julia Armfield wrote the perfect book for ya. . . . Armfield breaks your heart over and over (but in a good way, promise)."
—*Cosmopolitan*

"A love story like no other . . . Armfield's fantastic first novel is about the pockets of unknowability that pop up in even the longest intimacies, how marriage, like the ocean, is full of 'the teeth it keeps half-hidden.'"
—*Electric Literature*

"*Our Wives Under the Sea* meditates on whether it is possible to share the full truth of our hearts with others, what it means to leave, and, most of all, what it means to stay."
—*Literary Hub*

Our Wives
Under the Sea

JULIA ARMFIELD

FLATIRON
BOOKS
NEW YORK

OUR WIVES UNDER THE SEA. Copyright © 2022 by Julia Armfield. All rights reserved. Printed in the United States of America. For information, address Flatiron Books, 120 Broadway, New York, NY 10271.

www.flatironbooks.com

Designed by Susan Walsh

The Library of Congress has cataloged the hardcover edition as follows:

Names: Armfield, Julia, author.
Title: Our wives under the sea / Julia Armfield.
Description: First U.S. edition. | New York : Flatiron Books, [2022]
Identifiers: LCCN 2021047800 | ISBN 9781250229892 (hardcover) |
    ISBN 9781250229885 (ebook)
Subjects: LCGFT: Novels.
Classification: LCC PR6101.R638 O97 2022 | DDC 823/.92—dc23
LC record available at https://lccn.loc.gov/2021047800

ISBN 978-1-250-22990-8 (trade paperback)

Our books may be purchased in bulk for promotional, educational, or business use. Please contact your local bookseller or the Macmillan Corporate and Premium Sales Department at 1-800-221-7945, extension 5442, or by email at MacmillanSpecialMarkets@macmillan.com.

Originally published in the United Kingdom in 2022 by Picador, an imprint of Pan Macmillan

First published in the U.S. by Flatiron Books in 2022

First Flatiron Books Paperback Edition: 2023

10   9

For Rosalie, on dry land and elsewhere

Consider the subtleness of the sea; how its most dreaded creatures glide under water, unapparent for the most part, and treacherously hidden beneath the loveliest tints of azure. Consider also the devilish brilliance and beauty of many of its most remorseless tribes, as the dainty embellished shape of many species of sharks. Consider, once more, the universal cannibalism of the sea; all whose creatures prey upon each other, carrying on eternal war since the world began.

Consider all this; and then turn to the green, gentle, and most docile earth; consider them both, the sea and the land; and do you not find a strange analogy to something in yourself? For as this appalling ocean surrounds the verdant land, so in the soul of man there lies one insular Tahiti, full of peace and joy, but encompassed by all the horrors of the half-known life. God keep thee! Push not off from that isle, thou canst never return!

—*Moby-Dick*

ELLEN BRODY: There's a clinical name for it, isn't there?
MARTIN BRODY: Drowning.

—*Jaws*

Sunlight Zone

MIRI

The deep sea is a haunted house: a place in which things that ought not to exist move about in the darkness. *Unstill* is the word Leah uses, tilting her head to the side as if in answer to some sound, though the evening is quiet—dry hum of the road outside the window and little to draw the ear besides.

"The ocean is unstill," she says, "farther down than you think. All the way to the bottom, things move." She seldom talks this much or this fluently, legs crossed and gaze toward the window, the familiar slant of her expression, all her features slipping gently to the left. I'm aware, by now, that this kind of talk isn't really meant for me, but is simply a conversation she can't help having, the result of questions asked in some closed-off part of her head. "What you have to understand," she says, "is that things can thrive in unimaginable conditions. All they need is the right sort of skin."

We are sitting on the sofa, the way we have taken to doing in the evenings since she returned last month. In the old days, we used to sit on the rug, elbows up on the coffee table like teenagers, eating dinner with the television on. These days she rarely eats dinner, so I prefer to eat mine standing up in the kitchen to save on mess. Sometimes, she will watch me eat and when she does this I chew everything to a paste and stick my tongue out until she stops looking. Most nights, we don't talk—silence like a spine through the new shape our relationship has taken. Most nights, after eating, we sit together on the sofa until midnight, then I tell her I'm going to bed.

When she talks, she always talks about the ocean, folds her hands together and speaks as if declaiming to an audience quite separate from me. "There are no empty places," she says, and I imagine her glancing at cue cards, clicking through slides. "However deep you go," she says, "however far down, you'll find something there."

I used to think there was such a thing as emptiness, that there were places in the world one could go and be alone. This, I think, is still true, but the error in my reasoning was to assume that alone was somewhere you could go, rather than somewhere you had to be left.

It's three o'clock and I'm tilting the phone receiver away from my ear to avoid the hold music, which appears to be Beethoven's Battle Symphony played on a toy synthesizer. The kitchen is a junkyard of coffee cups, drain clogged with tea bags. One of the lights above the cooker hood is flickering— muscle pulse in the corner of my vision like a ticking eyelid. On the counter, the following: an orange, half-peeled; two knives; a plastic bag of bread. I haven't yet made lunch, pulled various items out at random about an hour ago before finding myself unequal to the task. Stuck to the fridge, a sheet of paper with the shopping list scratched down in purple Biro: *milk, cheese, sleep aid (any), sticking plasters, table salt.*

The hold music buzzes on and I probe around the inside of my mouth with my tongue, feel the gaps in my teeth the way I tend to do when I'm waiting for something. One of my molars is cracked, an issue I have been ignoring for some weeks because it doesn't seem to be hurting enough to warrant a fuss. I draw my tongue up over the tooth, feel the rise and split where the break runs along the enamel. *Don't do that*, I imagine Leah saying—the way she used to do when I rolled my tongue between my teeth in public—*you look like you forgot to floss*. Most nights, though I don't mention this to Leah, I dream in molars spat across the bedclothes, hold my hands beneath my chin to catch the teeth that drop like water from the lip of a tap. The general tempo of these dreams is always similar: the grasp and pull at something loose, the pause, the sudden fountain spill. Each time, the error seems to lie in the fact that I shouldn't have touched my fingers to the molar on the bottom left-hand side. Each time: the wrong switch flicked, my curiosity rewarded by a rain of teeth, too many to catch between two palms and force into my mouth again, my gums a bald pink line beneath my lip.

The line sputters, a recorded voice interrupting the music to tell me for the fiftieth time that my call is important, before the Battle Symphony recommences with what feels like renewed hostility. Across the room, Leah sits with her hands around a mug of water—a curious warming gesture, the way one might cradle a cup of tea. She hasn't drunk anything hot since returning, asked me not to make my coffee too near her, since the smell from the percolator now seems to make her gag. *Not to worry*, she has said more than once, *it'll sort itself. These things usually do*. Sensations are difficult still—touch painful, smells and tastes like small invasions. I've seen Leah touch her tongue to the edge of a piece of toast and retract it, face screwed up as if in response to something tart.

"I'm still on hold," I say, for no reason really other than to have said it. She looks at me, slow blink. *In case you were wondering*, I think of adding and don't.

At around six this morning, Leah woke and immediately had a nosebleed. I've been sleeping in the room across the hall and so didn't actually see this but I've grown accustomed to her patterns, even at this state of half remove. I'd been ready for it, had actually woken at six fifteen, in time to pass her a flannel in the bathroom, run the taps, and tell her not to put her head back. You could set your watch to it these days—red mouth in the morning, red chin, red spill into the sink.

She says, when she says anything, that it's something to do with the pressure, the sudden lack thereof. Her blood retains no sense of the boundaries it once recognized and so now just flows wherever it wants. Sometimes she bleeds from the teeth, or rather, not from the teeth but from the gums around the teeth, which amounts to the same thing when you're looking at her. In the days immediately following her return, blood would rise unheeded through her pores, so that sometimes I'd come in and find her pincushioned, dotted red, as if pricked with needles. *Iron maiden*, she'd said the first time and tried to laugh—strained sound, like the wringing out of something wet.

I found the whole thing terrifying for the first few days; panicked when she bled, jammed my shoes on and demanded she let me take her to A&E. Only by degrees did I realize she had been led to expect this, or at least to expect something similar. She pushed my hands from her face in a manner that seemed almost practiced and told me it wasn't a problem. *You can't go out in those anyway, Miri*, she said, looking down at the shoes I'd forced on without looking, *they don't match*.

On more than one occasion, I begged her to let me help her

and met only resistance. *You don't have to worry*, she would say, and then go on bleeding, and the obviousness of the problem combined with the refusal of help left me at first frustrated and subsequently rather resentful. It went on too long and too helplessly. The way that anyone who sneezes more than four times abruptly loses the sympathy of an audience, so it was with me and Leah. *Can't you stop it*, I'd think about asking her, *you're ruining the sheets.* Some mornings, I'd want to accuse her of doing it on purpose and then I'd look away, set my mouth into another shape, and pour the coffee, think about going for a run.

In the bathroom, just this morning, I passed her the flannel and watched her smear her hands with Ivory soap. My mother used to say that washing your face with soap was as bad as leaving it dirty, something about harsh chemicals, the stripping down of natural oils. Everything with my mother was always harsh chemicals—she filled a binder with clippings on the cancer risks of various meat products, sent me books on UV rays and home invasions, a pamphlet on how to build a fire ladder out of sheets.

Having washed her face, Leah stepped back from the sink. She patted her face with the backs of her hands, then the palms, then abruptly curled one finger into the lid beneath her left eye, then the right, pulling down to inspect the oily sockets of her eyeballs. In the mirror, her skin had the look of something dredged from water. The yellow eyes of someone drowned, of someone found floating on her back. *Be all right*, she said, *be all right in a minute.*

Now, in the kitchen: a jumbling noise on the phone. A sudden click and another robotic voice, slightly different from the one that has been repeating that my call is important, comes on the line to demand that I enter Leah's personnel number, followed by her rank number, transfer number, and the statement number she should have received from the Centre on final demob. The voice goes on to explain that if I fail to enter these numbers in the exact order required, I will be cut off. I do not, as I have been attempting to get through and explain, have Leah's personnel number—the whole purpose of my calling the Centre has been to try to get hold of it. I enter all the details required, aside from the personnel number, at which point a third recorded voice comes on the line and proceeds to scold me in a tight robotic jabber, noting as a helpful afterthought that my call will now be terminated.

LEAH

Did you know that until very recently, more people had been to the moon than had dived beyond depths of six thousand meters? I think about this often—the inhospitableness of certain places. A footprint, once left on the surface of the moon, might in theory remain as it is almost indefinitely. Uneroded by atmosphere, by wind or by rain, any mark made up there could quite easily last for several centuries. The ocean is different, the ocean covers its tracks.

When a submarine descends, a number of things have to happen in a fairly short span of time. Buoyancy is entirely dictated by water pushing up against an object with a force proportional to the weight of the water that object has displaced. So, when a submarine sits at the surface, its ballast tanks are filled with air, rendering its overall density less than that of the surrounding water (and thereby displacing less of it). In order to sink, those ballast tanks have to be filled with water, which is sucked into the vessel by electric pumps as the air is simultaneously forced out. It's a curious act of surrender, when you think about it, the act of going under. To drop below the surface is still to sink, however intentionally—a simple matter of taking on water, just as drowning only requires you to open your mouth.

Miri used to call these my *sunken thoughts*, tapping on the base of my skull with the flat of her hand when I grew quiet, frowning at some thought I was chasing in circles. *How'd they get so far down in there?* she'd say. *Next thing you know they'll be halfway down your neck.* When she did this, I would often catch her palm and keep it there, take her other hand and hold it to my temple, as though surrendering the responsibility of keeping my head in one piece.

It's hard to describe the smell of a submarine when it goes under. Hard to pin down—something like metal and hot grease and something like lack of oxygen, ammonia, the smell of all but what's necessary filtered away. Twenty minutes before we lost contact, Jelka told me she thought she smelled meat, which was strange, because I'd been thinking the same thing—a hot unsavory waft like something cooked. I remember I looked to my own fingers, half expected to find them roasting, bent to observe the skin on my shins, on my knees, on my ankles. There was nothing, of course, and no reason at all for the smell that seemed to hit us both with such force. When Jelka repeated her claim to Matteo, he told her to hold her nose if she was so bothered and I didn't say anything to back her up.

At first it was only the comms panel, the crackle of contact from the surface cutting out and not returning. I remember Matteo frowned and asked me to try to find a signal while he dealt with the main controls. I held down the transmission button and chanted nonsense into the radio, expecting the Centre to come back online any second and ask me what I was on about. Ten minutes later, when the craft's whole system went off-line, it would occur to me that the comms hadn't faded like a wavering signal so much as been switched off, though by that time we all had more pressing things to deal with.

MIRI

*She's been home three weeks and I'm mostly used to every-*thing. In the mornings, I eat and she doesn't and then I answer emails for half an hour and ignore her wandering back and forth with wads of toilet paper wedged along her gumline to absorb the blood. I write grant applications for nonprofit organizations for a living, and I've always worked from home, which never bothered me particularly until she went away and forced me into closer proximity with myself. Now that she's back—now I'm *used* to her being back—I can't decide whether to register her presence as relief or invasion. I make heavy weather over glasses left half-empty on windowsills, over the bin not being taken out. I have near-constant mouth ulcers and complain about unhoovered floors. At night, I dream I grit my teeth so hard that they break off like book matches.

The people who live above us keep the TV on at all times. Even when I know they're both out, at work or at the movies, the noise bleeds through the ceiling—downward drip of talk, of title music, spilling down the wall like the damp that speckles into mold around the chimney breast.

Sometimes, if I listen very closely (sometimes, if I stand on a chair), I can make out the show that's playing upstairs and tune our television to the same channel, which negates the irritation a little. They seem to favor game shows and programs about people tasked with falling in love with each other in exotic locations for money. I enjoy these, too, I suppose, enjoy their fabulism, the lunar tones of teeth. Contestants on a show I often watch in tandem with the neighbors have to stare into a stranger's eyes for four minutes, uninterrupted, as studies have apparently shown this is the amount of time it takes to fall in love. This often seems to work, at least for the duration of the episode, though once a male contestant threw his chair back after two minutes and walked off the set, later stating that something he saw in his partner had unnerved him. I'm less fond of nature documentaries and tend not to bother matching my channel to the neighbors' when they switch these on. One evening, I fell asleep on the sofa and woke to the unusually clear sound of a voice narrating a program on California pitcher plants from the floor above me: *Foraging insects are attracted to the cavity—or mouth—formed by the cupping of the leaf and are hastened down into the trap by the slippery rim kept moist by naturally occurring nectar. Once caught, the insect is drowned in the plant's digestive juices and gradually dissolved.* This was some months after Leah was first absent, when the phone calls from the Centre were still semiregular—the kindish, professional-sounding voices telling me they were doing all they could. I remember I lay on the sofa and listened to the show for several minutes before reaching for the remote and aiming it at the ceiling.

Leah used to go up there sometimes, knock on the door late at night, and ask them to turn it down. *They were nice,* she would tell me when she came back, brushing her hands together to indicate a job well done. *Very apologetic about it, I like them.* They left the TV on at night to keep the cat company, they'd turn it down, no harm no foul. The noise from the television never altered but I don't think Leah even particularly minded this. Going up there seemed, to her, to be almost the whole point of the exercise, telling the neighbors to turn it down more important than the turning down itself. After she went away, I quickly became grateful for a noise I had previously regarded as irritating. Sunday mornings I would stand on the kitchen table and listen to soap opera music, to upbeat voices selling nasal sprays and Lyle's Golden Syrup and non-stick Teflon pans.

"I can't stand this," Leah says suddenly. She's been sitting in the corner of the room for upward of an hour, chewing on the collar of her jumper in an odd, reflexive gesture, like one might gnaw at a hangnail. I ask her what she means and she doesn't say anything, only gesturing upward as the noise from the neighbors' television fades from the closing credits of a program to a splash of advert music in a frantic major key. I go upstairs and hammer on the door, but the neighbors don't answer, the noise of the television oddly quieter in the corridor than it seems in the flat below. It occurs to me that I have never actually laid eyes on the neighbors, that the whole time we've lived where we live I've taken their presence as a given on the basis of evidence that is, at best, circumstantial: the footsteps and the muffled music, scrape of furniture being moved around at night. I never asked Leah a single thing about the neighbors, never once after any of the times she went up to ask them to turn it down. *Is that odd?* I start to wonder to myself and then disregard the question. It barely matters, after all, since my issue is not so much with my neighbors as it is with their TV.

I'm only gone a total of six minutes but by the time I get back, Leah has moved from the corner of the living room and is locked in the bathroom, running both taps. This isn't entirely unusual. Quite often these days I will wake at odd hours and hear the bathtub being filled. Four A.M., gray twitch of morning in the sky about the telephone wires and water running in the bathroom, in the kitchen, in the room where the washer-dryer sits. More than once, I have come in to find Leah sitting on the edge of the bathtub, staring into the water with the fixed expression of someone barely awake. She is, as I often think at these moments, deliberating whether or not to get in, though at other times I interpret her expression as something more uneasy—the look of a person who has let their gaze drop too deep and now can't seem to retrieve it.

Standing outside the bathroom, I think of knocking, think of asking her to let me in. I imagine I can hear the water spilling down across the floor, pooling thick across the lavender linoleum. She has, it appears, taken the electric box she uses to sleep into the bathroom, the one that arrived in the post, no return address—a parting gift from the Centre—along with a pair of decompression socks and a book of aphorisms bound in PVC. I hear her turn it on, hear the shiver of sound it produces—swell and *oom* of something spilling, something seething, judder and groan of something building to a roar.

A long time ago, we met. I think that's important—the fact of a meeting, the fact I remember a sense of before. Meeting implies a point before knowing, a point before Leah and I became this fused, inextricable thing. We used to make a game of remembering, elbowing each other about it: *d'you remember the time I sent flowers when you were living in another city, d'you remember teaching me to swim, d'you remember the time we went out for my birthday and you spilled water all over the table and the waiter looked at us like we'd crawled from a hole in the ground.* Every couple, I think, enjoys its own mythology, recollections like note cards to guide you around an exhibition: *Fig. A. Portrait of the couple dancing at a colleague's Catholic wedding. Fig. B. Charcoal sketch of the couple fighting over who said what at a cokey dinner with acquaintances (note fine lines beneath completed sketch, indicating places where the artist has repeatedly erased and redrawn).* Things are easy enough to recall, in isolation. Scenes appear complete unto themselves: the time we went to the fancy dress party, the time someone stole my wallet in a club, the time our train carriage got stuck underground for an hour and forty-five minutes and Leah kept hold of my hand until we started to move. You can wander the exhibition this way, picking favorites, placing dots by the frames of the pictures you most want to keep. Trickier is the task of pulling the pictures together, of connecting the points in a way that makes tangible sense. I remember the first time we kissed, the first time we slept together, the first time she told me she'd once seen her father appear at the foot of her bed as a ghost. I remember fucking—or the abstract sense of fucking—the fact of doing it often and cheerfully, though with little recollection of one time over the next. I remember the first time she went away, the first time I traveled to see her off. I remember the last time—the fact that she was supposed to be gone for three weeks and disappeared for six months, the fact that none of us knew what had happened, the way the Centre called several times to give out contradictory information before ceasing to call at all. All of this is easy enough, at close range—bright flashes, a relationship borne out by evidence, the bits and pieces that make it a fact. What is harder is stepping back far enough to consider us in the altogether, not the series of pictures but the whole that those pictures represent. I don't particularly like to do this. Stepping back too far makes me dizzy—my memory, like something punched, reeling about with its hands clapped over its face. It is easier, I think, to consider the fact of us in its many disparate pieces, as opposed to one vast and intractable thing. Easier, I think, to claw through the scatter of us in the hopes of retrieving something, of pulling some singular thing from the debris and holding it up to the light.

So in pieces, then: a long time ago, we met.

LEAH

Panic is a misuse of oxygen. The first thing anyone learns in diving is how to breathe. When the console lights went off, I held my breath for a full sixty seconds, considered the wet wing-shapes of my lungs. There is a practice in Norse mythology that involves the severing of the ribs from the spinal column and the lungs being drawn from the back, extracted in such a manner that the victim is supposedly still able to breathe. Variously described as a method of torture and a means of human sacrifice, there is some debate as to whether this was ever actually performed outside of literature. It would be impossible, of course, to do so with the victim still alive—the lungs wouldn't function outside of the body, and even if they did, the victim would most likely go into shock and stop breathing on their own. Even so, one can think of the lungs sometimes and believe it. Picture their wide, whaling chambers, the bald imperative of all they are made to contain. I don't know why I'm mentioning this, really, except that this is what I thought about in the sixty seconds between the system dying and the next breath I was able to take. I thought about my lungs being wrenched through my back and still swelling, contracting, thought of water spilling into the space where my rib cage had been and my lungs going on regardless.

At this point, I should note, we were still following protocol, at least to some degree. It is actually very rare for a submarine to sink, but there are guidelines in place for this eventuality as there are for all things, the most vital of which is to send a distress call without delay. The earlier you can do this (and the closer to the surface you are when you do), the more likely it is that a coastguard or passing vessel will pick up the signal and realize that something is wrong. The problem, of course, is that sending a distress call relies on your system being online, which ours was not. I remember Matteo at the comms panel, moving his hands over the console for a moment and then looking at me. I remember, too, the disquieting lack of electric light—the switches dull—the way our craft seemed suddenly less a piece of precision-tooled engineering and more a swiftly sinking box. Matteo was the one who checked the engines, the junction boxes, the pressure gauges. "There's nothing wrong," he said. "It should all be working fine."

We were still descending when the system went out and already too deep to evacuate. Our CO_2 scrubbers, for whatever reason, appeared to have remained intact, but with no way to control the ballast tanks, there was nothing we could do but continue to drop.

MIRI

I hold the phone to my collarbone and yell for Leah. I don't typically like to raise my voice, but the sound of running water has taken on the ubiquity of traffic in our flat and I have to shout sometimes just to make myself heard. The woman on the line has asked to speak to the authorized personnel directly, as she cannot deal with me on Leah's behalf.

"But I have all the numbers," I say, "you know the reason I'm calling—why can't you just deal with me?"

It has taken six separate attempts on six different days to get through to a real person, and the elation of this has unfortunately led me to overestimate the extent to which a real person is actually going to be able to help.

"I'm afraid I can't do that," the real person says now. "I can only speak about company matters with the authorized personnel."

I open my mouth, close it, try again.

"But she's my wife. I have all her details. What if I just pretended to be her. Would that be OK?" The real person makes an awkward little noise.

"I'm afraid I can't do that." The sound of running water continues. I consider shouting for Leah again and don't.

"I could put the phone down and call you back and do a different voice, if you liked? I'll say it's Leah from the start, that way you won't get into trouble. You just tell anyone who asks that I'm her and it's fine, I swear."

There is a curious noise on the line—I can't tell if the real person is sighing or crying or eating a sandwich.

"I'm afraid I can't do that, Miri."

A thin needling rain, like someone is throwing pins from the rooftops. On the sofa, Leah pours cherry Coke into a plastic glass patterned with hamburgers and then does not drink it, glides her fingers down the skin of her left arm. She is silvered over, oystered at her elbow creases and around the neck. This is something I noticed when she first came back and wasn't sure how to bring up, though she pointed it out herself before too long: *Look at this, and this, they told us to expect some stuff like that.*

It'll go away, she says, not so much to me as to herself. Just another reaction, a thing to be dismissed, like the bleeding, like the way she sometimes sleepwalks to the bathroom and holds her head under the water, having first filled the bath to a point just shy of overflowing. She doesn't know that the first time I noticed the change in her skin, I was so alarmed that I called 111 and hung on the line for thirty minutes, only for someone to finally come on and ask if I'd ever heard of impetigo.

"You don't need to look at me like that," she says now, still moving her fingers along the skin of her arm. "I can feel your look," she adds when I open my mouth to say something. "But you don't need to. It's OK."

"I'm not looking at you in any special way," I say, in a voice that aims for a joke and misses. She gives me a sideways look, starts to smile and then doesn't entirely.

"OK," she says. "So you're not looking at me. My mistake."

The conversation, brief as it is, is a welcome break in the

silence, though the silence resettles shortly afterward, some-how heavier than before. I have found myself trying to escape this new lack between us, grown conscientious about my run-ning, lingering hours in the supermarket, pointlessly deliberat-ing over brands of detergent, scrutinizing tubs of yogurt and butter and butter substitute. Occasionally, I will tell Leah I'm leaving the flat to complete a specific activity and instead sim-ply walk to some fixed point and stand there until I get bored enough to return. I don't think I'm even particularly clever about this. *You said you were going to the gym,* she'll say to me sometimes, *but you didn't take any kit with you.* I'll tell her she misheard me and she will accept it, going back to staring at a point on her inner arm or to running the taps in the kitchen until the sink fills up.

In the supermarket, then. Carmen squints at cans of chopped tomatoes, raises and lowers packets of differently shaped pasta. She has left her glasses in the office and can't see the number of fingers I'm holding up if I stand more than a foot away.

"What's this?" she asks, holding up a parcel of orecchiette. "Is this the one that looks like ears?"

We've been friends since university but her eyesight only really started to deteriorate over the past year or so. It went downhill so suddenly that she went to the doctor about it, make-believing brain tumors, gray shadows on X-ray print-outs of her skull. This has always been the chief point over which our friendship has endured—the hypochondriac back and forth of two women with too much time on their hands. We've talked each other down from any number of ledges—from Carmen's meningitis panic to my generalized fears around cancer and Alzheimer's and diseases I'm concerned I might catch or inherit—though when Carmen's eyesight started failing I was too busy to help her as much as I should have, and I feel that between us a little now.

"So how's it going?" she asks later, the two of us folded over coffees, our hair identically greased by the rain and fizzing out around our temples. The café is one we visit often, and familiarity has become a key concern for Carmen, just lately. I watch her fumble her way to the counter and back, her long hands running over the Perspex cake cabinet, twin smears that will need to be wiped away.

"It's fine," I say, carving my initials through latte foam with a teaspoon handle. "It's strange, you know, but it's fine."

"I guess it must be weird," she says—the sweet plum of her voice, the way her vowels seem to take up more space than the shape of her mouth allows—"living with someone again after such a long absence. I guess it must be weird," she says, "having to share your space."

I look at her, open my mouth to tell her that's not what I meant at all. *Living with someone again*, I want to say, *isn't what it feels like.*

"When I moved in with Tom," she carries on, unable, I suppose, to read the fact of my open mouth, "it was so weird for so long—like it felt such an invasion, you know? Like you love someone but that doesn't mean you want to be with them *all the time*, you know? Like sometimes I'd lock myself in the bathroom and just lie in the bath for half an hour—not with the water running, I mean, just in the empty bath—just because it was the only way I could get some *space*. And I *loved* him, you know? So I really do get the disconnect."

Carmen's ex-boyfriend Tom was a social worker and weekend DJ who eventually left her for reasons I never quite managed to grasp. Carmen typically speaks about him the way one might refer to a degree: a three-year period one has to endure in order to talk with overbearing authority on exactly one subject. She is the world's living expert on loving and losing thirty-year-old men named Tom.

"It's not really that so much," I say, turning my head toward the window so she can't follow the expression on my face. The rain has picked up. "I never minded sharing the space. That felt like the whole point of living together."

Later on, walking home, I stop at the petrol station and buy another cherry Coke to replace the one Leah wasted earlier in the day. I stand in the car park and watch the sky growing dark beyond the tower blocks, the buildings like faces buried in unclean pillows. We have always lived here—met in a pale electric summer, moved quickly from our respective basement studios to the second-floor flat we have shared for seven years. Before she transferred to the Centre, Leah used to take the train each morning, an hour at least to run her out through brown uncertain marshlands to the research facility, minutes from the sea. An hour back in again at night, her clothes salt-glazed, her skin scoured smooth by coastal weather. Strange, to live in such proximity to an ocean that I almost never see.

The city is veined with inland tributaries and close-dispersed canals, waterlogged about its edges. Bridged across its belly, a river running down its throat. August in the city is always strange, wet, scuttled through with insects freshly burst from shells. I scratch my calf with the toe of my left shoe and think about Leah—about her bright pale eyes and the shape of her mouth and the feeling when we spoke for the first time that there were vast places in the world that I had never yet thought to go.

A thousand years ago, Leah held a hand over my mouth in the bathroom at the wedding of a mutual friend. We'd gone into the stall together because I needed help with the buttons up the back of my jumpsuit and had ended up trapped when one of the bridesmaids came in and started sobbing to someone on the phone.

It was roughly five o'clock, fireworks planned for seven thirty and rain forecast for six. *I just don't think*, the bridesmaid wailed into her mobile, *that it's such a big deal when I've been carrying her fucking spare shoes around with me all day. I just don't think that it's so much to ask, to be understanding, when I handmade those fucking centerpieces myself.*

In the stall, I pictured the bridesmaids: six of them, goosefleshed in summer dresses. During the ceremony, they had stood in line as if in preparation for a hanging, the sense of a barely under control Salem implicit in their fixed expressions, in the mess of arms that later reached toward the bride at the behest of the wedding photographer: *We're doing a funny one now—act like you all want to choke her!*

Leah gave me a warning look that tumbled off into a smile, pressing her hand down harder to stop me from laughing. *I'm just so tired*, the bridesmaid sighed—the plink of earrings removed and dropped into the sink—*I just can't believe she's so angry at me because I—oh—right, yes of course, I'm sorry. Absolutely, go if you have to go.* She dissolved into fresh sobs and I watched Leah's face change a little, her typical reaction to genuine suffering always being to cease laughing before I did and then look at me until I stopped. I rolled my eyes at her and she pulled her hand away from my mouth, murmured *come on* before easing the bathroom door open. The bridesmaid by the sink had apparently suffered a catastrophically unexpected period, the lavender silk of her dress streaked red all up the back. *Hey*, Leah said, and the bridesmaid jumped and turned and then carried on crying, and Leah told her not to worry and then listened to her sob for twenty minutes while I sat beside the sink and handed over a pound for the tampon machine.

Later on, fireworks called off because of rain, Leah went out to the covered porch and I went with her. Across the courtyard, a view of the rest of the venue—wide white outbuildings arranged in a semicircle. Georgian by design, it had apparently been used as the primary setting for a recent Austen adaptation on a midbudget cable channel—cardboard cutouts of the hero and heroine standing life-size in the reception area, sun-faded toward the end of the tourist season. For all its photogenic lines, the house retained little of its original features beyond a tottering cupola and a widow's walk made semilethal with age. A folly, so the receptionist had explained unprompted when we first arrived: *Widow's walks are typically a feature of coastal dwellings. Wives would watch for their husbands' ships, mothers for their sons— fishing boats, whalers, smugglers. And there was always the possibility of pirates. Things to look out for. Not so helpful sixty miles inland.*

Back inside, the previously distraught bridesmaid was now dancing, having tied her boyfriend's suit jacket around her waist to cover the stain. *That's sweet*, Leah had said when she saw the boyfriend offering the jacket and I had grinned at her without really knowing why. *I'll do that for you*, she had added, *next time you have a terrible period and I'm wearing a suit.*

On the porch, I took her hand and we stood like that for a while, saying nothing. It occurred to me to joke that when we got married, I wouldn't want anyone to worry about bleeding through their dresses, that when we got married I'd be offended if everyone didn't menstruate freely all over the place. I didn't say this, as we hadn't yet officially talked about getting married, and anyway, the quiet was as nice as anything else.

I guess it must be weird, Carmen had said, having to share your space. I think about this a lot in the gaps where my and Leah's conversation ought to be. At dinner, leaning up against the counter, my tongue swells with it, my throat and palate clenching vainly around the lack. We say nothing to each other—I ask her if she wants to eat, she tells me no, she asks me what I'm drinking, but still, in a very fundamental sense, we say nothing. Even her reassurances about the blood, about the places where her skin has changed color, are starting to fade away. Sometimes, I imagine the things I want to say to her, but increasingly I find myself capable of producing little but a kind of mental white noise. My brain moves like a jump between radio stations, falling off topics without warning, cutting to music, to adverts, to weather. I go about my work, chop onions, overseason my food. Every so often, I imagine I hear the neighbors' television prompting me to speak, although on these occasions it's typically just a game show host inviting a contestant to answer a question before the time runs out.

One morning, I read a newspaper article about a Korean woman who ate improperly prepared seafood and subsequently went to the doctor complaining of a growth on the inside of her cheek. The doctor, assuming a cyst or fibrous tu-

mor, ordered a biopsy, but on opening her up they found nothing to indicate cancer. Instead, embedded inside the growth,
they found the bodies of twelve tiny organisms, squirmed
with suckers, each a little over a centimeter in length. So it
transpired, the squid that this woman had eaten had been prepared without first having its organs removed. The woman, or
more specifically her buccal mucosa, had thus become unwit-
ting host to a dozen squid paralarvae—minute creatures that,
on removal, the doctor thoughtfully placed in a fluid preserva-
tive and gave to the woman to take home.

"Listen to this," I say, reading aloud from the kitchen table
without exactly meaning to. *"On first discovering the paralarvae,
Dr. Shim was heard to remark that he would be canceling the sushi
he had ordered for lunch.* That's funny," I say. "Don't you think
that's funny?"

Leah is sitting across the table, staring at some point just
north of my head. When I nudge my foot against hers, she
blinks, her expression that of someone who's been pulled from
some more practical task. I spread the paper out on the table
between us, point out the pictures that accompany the article.
In the first, a woman holds up the jam jar into which she has
decanted her specimens, the ossified little bodies in their green-
ish liquid reminding me oddly of the sea monkeys I begged for
my eighth birthday and never received. The caption beneath
the picture: *Ms. Moon presents her offspring.* The second photograph shows the doctor who performed the biopsy posing
incongruously before a wall of white hydrangeas. I squint at
the two photographs, replaying the article like a fairy story
and imagining the patient and doctor going on to fall in love
and marry, bridesmaids strewing a wet confetti of squid eggs
at their wedding.

"Do you think she felt better with those things out of her," Leah asks and I look at her—tight, piercing thrill of her saying something, like a needle forced through skin. I look at her for a moment, the long neck and back and all of her leaning down over the newspaper, two fingers pinched around the head of the doctor in the photograph, as though attempting to pry it off. I poke my tongue into my mouth and try to imagine such a haunting, of prying open Leah's mouth and finding something pressed against the backs of her teeth. I want to tell her it should all come out, every piece of it—bad cells extracted from her body. I want to tell her that it has to feel better to be rid of it. In the end, however, I only shrug, still squinting at the photo of the woman with her jar of tiny bodies—the tight bouquets of tentacles and fleshy white mantles, a convention of sheeted ghosts.

"Who knows," I say. "Think of the inside of someone's mouth. All that squelching dark. I'd expect they were gladder to be shot of her."

"What would you have done if you'd found something like that in your mouth?"

She is looking at me seriously now. I think about my own mouth, imagine it filled with things that have no business being there—ghost groans of words that died before my tongue could shape them.

"If I found something like that in my mouth, I'd spit it out."

We used to watch movies—it was our thing, our first obvious point of connection. Our first dates revolved around it—watching movies by Cronenberg and Bava alone in cinemas emptied out by summer weather, Leah's shoulder damp against my own and the scuffle of mice in dark places, behind the screen and along the backs of our chairs. In the evenings after these dates, we would wander together, arguing about *Shivers* and *The Fly*, about whether or not a movie even counted as a date if it didn't come attendant on dinner. The first time Leah stayed over at mine, we watched *Jaws* and afterward talked so long about how Hooper and Brody were obviously in love that we forgot to have sex and simply fell asleep together, Leah's ankle hooked over my hip. In the morning, she woke me up by playing the *Jaws* theme full volume in my ear.

(My friends often told me in these early days that we were similar, something I always thought bizarre, although Leah pointed out that all they meant by this was that we both talked fast and watched movies in the evenings after work. In truth, I never thought there were too many points of congruence between us. We were both small, though I was specifically short and Leah specifically skinny; we both hated loud noises and bad manners and enjoyed the peculiar clench of city space. Beyond that, there were few similarities. On occasion, particularly with friends like Carmen, it occurred to me that this perceived resemblance between Leah and myself had more to do with the two of us being women than it did with anything real. *You're just like twins*, Carmen said once. *I wish I had what you have.* I found myself wanting to point out that she and her boyfriend Tom actually had a lot in common, though this didn't seem a point on which she longed for me to press.)

I watch movies alone now—Leah's concentration is not what it used to be. When I can't sleep, which is often, I take myself out of the spare room and watch movies on the living room floor until the sky grows light beyond the telegraph poles and my back starts to hump from sitting so long with my arms curled over my knees. I watch only movies I've seen before—impossible, I think, to follow something new, to find the will to do so. I put *Jaws* on, once, although this turned out to be a mistake and I turned it off within the first ten minutes. The first time we watched that movie together, Leah went into great detail about all the ways she would have gone about catching the shark, about the technology available, the ways in which our ability to observe and understand marine life has advanced since the mid-1970s. After talking like this for several minutes, she suddenly grinned at me, cutting herself off and rolling her eyes to the ceiling—*but this is boring*, she said, *I don't want to be boring. We're watching a movie.* I shook my head and turned down the sound on the television. *No*, I said to her, *no, not boring at all.*

LEAH

Jelka prayed, because that was what Jelka did. Matteo said nothing, only checked and rechecked the oxygen systems and announced every time that we were fine, still fine, still breathing. I'm not entirely sure what I did. It occurred to me several times, in a mildly hysterical manner, that a submarine going down was not in itself a terrible thing. It occurred to me several times to say this—*What are we worried about, this is just what we're supposed to be doing!* I didn't say this, of course, only held my finger against the transmission button at ten-second intervals and registered dead signal each time. Typically, it should take a manned submersible craft anywhere between three and four hours to reach the deepest point in the ocean, depending on the size of the craft and its engines. I wondered, in a fairly distant way, what would happen when we hit the bottom and couldn't control the ballast tanks to bring us up again. I wondered how it was that the system had cut out in all meaningful ways except when it came to the CO_2 scrubbers. I wished, with a vehemence that felt vaguely misplaced, that I had thought to bring a deck of cards with me. I imagined the three of us sitting at the bottom of the ocean and playing old maid.

The deep sea is dark, particularly when the lights on your submersible craft have cut out for reasons unknown. I did my best to keep my gaze away from the windows, thought of strange-shaped ocean creatures peering in at the three of us and smiling with all of their teeth.

Twilight Zone

MIRI

There was a cocktail party to celebrate their going away; white wine and Twiglets held in a hotel conference room by the Centre for Marine Enquiry and three men in turquoise suits playing bossa nova music on a platform near the door. I spent much of the night caught up in interminable conversation with a man who specialized in seaweed (specialized in what sense I wasn't sure; he introduced himself as such and I didn't care to probe). *Which one is yours*, he asked at one point, gesturing toward the group that stood farthest from the buffet, as though asking me to identify my jacket from a pile. Leah was standing at the outer edge of the group, holding a glass and talking in a tone that seemed flushed through with bright authority, though I wasn't close enough to hear what she was actually saying. Her dress was white and clung to her like sealskin. She didn't often wear dresses, though when she did it always seemed she chose the ones that looked like something else: cocoons and folded paper, carapaces, wet suits, wings. Like an insect that mimics something else, at a distance it could often be hard to tell quite what it was that you were looking at. Dressing for formal events, I often thought of her like this: sheathing herself with the intent to deflect. She didn't much enjoy being looked at. *There's a lot of it about*, the seaweed specialist said when I pointed Leah out and explained what we were to each other. *My brother's wife has a sister, you know. Same thing.*

The venue was overbright, my mouth raw from hot coffee

drunk too quickly sometime that afternoon. A strange atmosphere—something like tension in the walls, in the way people spoke to each other. I felt stripped of too many of my senses, concerned about my rhythm, about the exact small sequence of movements required to put my hand on Leah's arm. Earlier in the evening we had fought, I forget about what exactly. Certainly not about her going away or any reservations I might have had about the trip. If it were possible now to look back and feel at least secure in the fact that I had predicted something, noted some foul planetary alignment and spoken my fears aloud, that might be of some comfort. As it was, I suspected nothing. Leah had gone and returned many times before and I had no reason to presume this trip would be any different. What we'd argued about had been something banal, impossible to recall and easy enough to guess at: Leah never wiping the surfaces down unless prompted, Leah never giving me two seconds just to stare into space without asking me what I was thinking. Very often, people argue as a way of expressing the fears and frustrations they cannot say aloud. It would, perhaps, be easy enough to claim that Leah's impending departure was what prompted me to pick fights unnecessarily and often, but to be perfectly honest I'm not certain that's what it was. Often enough it's occurred to me that fighting is simply something I'm given to, like picking at my cuticles. Whatever it was we fought about, the climax was loud, fraught, and quickly forgotten. We had never been very committed fighters—bit and scratched and then grew bored, too quick to appease and to declare ourselves the ones at fault. The problem with relationships between women is that neither one of you is automatically the wronged party, which frankly takes a lot of the fun out of an argument.

That night, the fight sat between us like something sore and satisfying—tender pulp of a fresh-pulled tooth. The sense of something better off removed. I felt good to have scrapped and apologized. Moving around the party, I registered the ache between us and felt grateful, irritable, loved her easily. She brought me a glass of something, pulled my hair from where it had slipped down the neck of my dress, kissed my temple, and snorted when a woman from the Centre introduced herself, despite having already spoken to me several times that night. *I'm sorry*, the woman said when Leah pointed this out to her, *one of those nights. It's all blah blah blah, hi hi hi, bullshit bullshit bullshit.* Leah explained that the two of them would be crewmates on the forthcoming expedition, that they had actually worked together before. I nodded and smiled and asked if she was looking forward to the trip. *As much as anyone looks forward to a long commute*, the woman replied, and Leah huffed a laugh, kept an arm around my shoulders. *Jelka thinks she's such a scream*, she said to me and Jelka shrugged and asked me what I did for work. I remember the way it felt to stand with the two of them, the way people turned to look at them, occasionally interrupting our conversation to shake their hands. *It's like you're famous*, I teased at one point and Jelka made a face. *That's just what these people are like*, she said, raising an eyebrow at Leah. *Weird. Weird people. Haven't I said this since we came to work here?* Leah laughed, leaned more heavily into my side. *You just like being mean about people*, she said, *there's nothing wrong with them at all.*

At the end of the night, there were toasts; well-wishes for the expedition, joking exhortations not to stay away too long. A woman waxed lyrical on advances in technology, on the research opportunities opened up by the Centre's commitment to modernity. The atmosphere, though convivial, seemed shot through with something unidentifiable—strange sensation, almost a flavor in the air. During the toasts, I saw several people from the Centre standing with hands clasped in front of them or under their chins, the way you might expect to witness at a church event. I stood with Leah and registered a sense of unzipping, turned my head into her neck and whispered that I was sorry about the fight.

I am reading a book I found in a charity shop, flipping through in the hopes of encountering notes made by previous owners, which is one of my favorite things to do. Leah used to buy me books chosen purely on the strength of this, presenting me with copies of *Das Kapital* and *Middlemarch* with inscriptions scrawled across their title pages by people I will never meet. *For Doreen, without apprehension. For Jack, on his birthday and despite his behavior.* The book I am reading is a textbook on human anatomy, coffee stained and sticky to the touch, long chunks of text irregularly underlined at points referring to nerve endings and dormant human tissue, as though the previous owner had been using it to build a monster in a shed. *Structurally,* I read aloud to myself, for no other reason than because it is underlined, *there are three classes of sensory receptors: free nerve endings, encapsulated nerve endings, and specialized cells. Free nerve endings are simply free dendrites at the end of a neuron that extend into a tissue. Pain, heat, and cold are all sensed through free nerve endings.*

Leah has been in the bathroom for upward of two hours, running the taps and listening to her sound machine, which fills the flat with a foaming swell of noise. I haven't asked her to come out this morning; I rolled over and refused to get up when I heard her at the sink at quarter past six. *Only today*, I told myself, pulled the pillow over my face and promised I would get up and help tomorrow. I have yet to get used to the spare room, puddle my clothes on the carpet with the affect of one returned to a childhood home for Christmas and reluctant to do any washing. There are glasses piled on the table beside the bed, sour with nighttime water, dust, drowned spiders. I have taken several books from their old spot in the bedroom and use them to hold the door ajar at night. I didn't take possession of the spare room immediately on Leah's return but rather moved across in a strop one night when Leah had kept me awake sleepwalking back and forth between bedroom and bathroom, lying down only to get up again. I had intended to stay in the spare room only one night and yet somehow never moved back. This is something I am, for the moment, not willing to examine too closely. Sometimes in the dark, I imagine I hear Leah knocking on the wall that separates us, neat little knocks that request not entry but only conversation. Not real, of course, but something to occupy my mind when my home seems to fill with water and I find myself without the correct materials to plug the gaps.

I have read the majority of the book on anatomy by the time I hear the bath begin to drain, the door open, and Leah padding out and back into the bedroom—wet feet on carpet, door click, and then quiet. I get up, the way I always do, and move across the corridor to scrub at the bath with the sponge I keep beneath the sink. I have found that since returning, Leah is prone to ring the bath with a scrim of some curiously viscous material, oddly gritty when rolled between finger and thumb and pinkish in the white bathroom light. When I look at it, I think of tide pools filled with spiny creatures, scrub at it before running the taps again to clear the debris, little rock pool remains of something that might be shell or might be skin or might be something else entirely. I squeeze the sponge out in the sink and stow it, wander back to the spare room, and think about doing some work.

———————

People grow odd when there's too much sky—they lose the sense of land around them, think themselves into floating away. When my mother was dying I wanted her moved somewhere other than where she was, wished her away from the wide bright vista that spilled into her room every morning, sending her—as I felt at the time—undeniably mad.

The house was built into a cliffside over the water, offering wide-open views across the tops, from the Dufflin copse that covered the headland to the Davey Elms that lined the ridge. The trees around her house were always bent down, stomach-ached in the wind, her windows smeared with the bodies of insects that hurled themselves against the glass in search of respite from the weather. She had lived by the sea for some seventeen years, largely alone except for when the nurse became essential. The medication eased involuntary movements, but increasingly there arose a danger of choking, of falling, of not being able to climb the stairs. She refused almost every aspect of my help, the way women will when they've been bred to accept little more than the basest civility. *Patronizing*, my mother used to say, when her hairdresser made a joke that veered toward the familiar, when a friend invited her to join her divorcees' coffee morning—*so she's saying I'm the kind of sad act who needs to hang around with other sad acts and weep into my tea until it's time to go home? Well, no thank you, chum, I'm quite happy on my own.* It was very easy to offend my mother. Rather in the way that it's very easy to kill an orchid, it often seemed little short of inevitable. Visiting her brought with it the implication that you regarded her as lonely, failing to visit her was an insult all its own. Birthday presents bore about a fifty-fifty chance of misconstrual. My mother: poring over a book on French revolutionary history, pulling a pair of jade earrings from a box, pursing her lips for a second and nodding—*I see*, as though she quite understands the insult.

Typically, when I visited, we spoke on only very general topics: my hair, the weather, what it was exactly that I did for work again. I loved her hard and at a distance, which made it easier to do, experienced brief but powerful compulsions to hug her and almost never did. She was ill for a long time—a white-knuckled, unbecoming illness that is also, as it happens, frequently passed down from parent to child. I sent my mother flowers and boxes of Jaffa Cakes and visited her less often than was kind. Toward the end of her illness, it became too difficult for her to live on her own and she was moved into full-time hospice care. I remember the day I moved her out—a sky like scalded milk, the smell of something burning. I remember the slip of skin between her knuckles, her white-blond hair, the heavy jewelry of bones too clear beneath the surface.

But perhaps not this just yet, actually. I'm not sure I have the stomach for it.

———

The sofa again, and Leah talking the way she does—not at me but at some point to the general left of me, soliloquizing at the wall.

"Some people," she says, "think the granite floor of the Pacific was torn away to make the moon. Darwin's son, actually. He said that. That when the Earth was young it rotated very quickly—it went so fast that part of it flew off into space, and the Pacific is the scar it left behind."

"Cool," I say. "I'm trying to watch television."

I sit where I am and don't look at her. She is wearing a tank top that shows the strange silvered places in her underarms and around the base of her neck and I no longer feel much compelled to comment on this. I find that if I squint at the television hard enough, it's easier to think about things other than how much I miss my wife.

LEAH

In the sea there's no such thing as a natural horizon, no place for the line of the sky to signify an end. When you sink—which we did, long hours of sinking—you can't see the bottom and you can't see the top and the ocean around you extends on both sides with no obvious limit except the border around your own window. Earth and its certain curvature become far less clear underwater.

Jelka stopped praying after the first hour and instead started humming, which was worse. I considered saying something and then willed myself to kindness. *How would you feel*, I thought, forgetting for a moment that I was in the exact same position as her. Technically speaking, there was nothing to fix and so no way we could go about fixing it. Matteo continued to batter vaguely at the console and I helped him, though this was not my job and wouldn't have had much effect even if it had been. At one point, Matteo caught his elbow on the corner of the comms deck and cursed, drawing up sharply and swearing he could break his neck in a fucking toy box craft like this. I clicked my tongue and told him to stop before he broke something worth actual money. I'm not sure why we behaved this way, to be honest. It feels odd, on reflection, to consider the very little we chose to do as we fell beyond diveable depths and still farther. I know it occurred to me, in a distant fashion, that an alarm ought to have gone off to alert us to a battery failure, however many hours ago. I know it occurred to me, too, that we'd need to release weights to slow our descent once we reached thirty-five thousand feet but now had no obvious way of doing that, nor any way of telling how far we'd dropped. It occurred to me that falling too fast and landing too suddenly—wherever we did eventually land—would surely result in a catastrophic rupture of the craft's outer shell, with upward of six miles of water on top of us. All of this occurred to me, certainly, but only at a kind of remove. It was like the dispassionate realization that one has left the house without first turning a light out—unfortunate but hardly a disaster. I don't remember thinking we would die, so much as noting that we wouldn't be able to come back up again. I don't remember thinking we could fix things, only wondering what would happen next.

At some point, Matteo brought out four wide electric torches and placed them around the base of the main deck. Since the console lights had failed, we'd been sitting in semidarkness, and in this fresh illumination, I looked about the craft the way one might peruse a Spot the Difference game—the same, but with deliberate mistakes. Same console, but with all the buttons dim; same machinery, only silent. Same Jelka, too, only hunched about the base of her chair, pulling quietly at the skin around her nails. Certain things, however, remained as I remembered them: Matteo's Cthulhu bobblehead suckered to the ledge beneath the main window, Jelka's rosary looped around the console stand the way you'd hang prayer beads from a rearview mirror. I remember thinking idly that we ought to have brought air freshener—hung the little pine-fresh trees like talismans around the deck.

"Do you think," I said at some point (I forget what point exactly), "that we ought to do something."

Neither of them said anything to this, although Matteo did begin to whistle, which was a weak advance on Jelka's humming. He whistled tunefully and through his teeth, *Farewell and adieu to you fair Spanish ladies*, swooning low about the tincan confines of the craft.

When I was seven, my father taught me to swim, by which I mean that he wrenched my knuckles from the side of the municipal swimming pool and hurled me into the deep end with a ruthlessness bordering on zealotry. *Just keep your head up*, he yelled, impassive to my shrieking and to the well-intentioned lifeguard who blew a feeble whistle twice and then gave up. Prior to this point, I had never been keen on the water, imagining only preying dark places and ocean floors that dropped suddenly away. My father, sensing pathology the way that bloodhounds catch a scent, had taken on my training as a kind of aversion therapy, and despite being the type of man to whom anxiety was only proof of thinking too hard, he had turned out to have the right idea. *If you've got breath enough to scream, you're not drowning* was his most frequent refrain, and inasmuch as that I had to learn to swim to avoid being fished from the bottom of the pool and taken directly to the coroner, his method basically worked. When explaining the divorce to me, I remember my mum said that it had always been next to impossible to tolerate a man whose approach to problem-solving was the psychological equivalent of a Wile E. Coyote–shaped hole in a canyon wall. That they were happier unshackled from one another was obvious, and I certainly enjoyed them both better the moment they stopped pretending to share any common goal beyond me. My father taught me to swim and later to scuba-dive, my mum bought me UltraSwim chlorine-removal shampoo. I grew used to the water in stages and then fell in love with it, read the books my father bought me on deep-sea exploration, dreamed in shoals of Humboldt squid and molten silverfish. I found I slept best to the telling of stories that flung me out onto the ocean, asked to be read to until I grew older and read the stories to myself. One of the stories I loved best was that of a man named Thor Heyerdahl, a Norwegian adventurer and ethnographer of the mid-1940s who once sailed five thousand miles across the Pacific in a hand-built raft crewed only by five men. Heyerdahl had nearly drowned at least twice in boyhood and did not take easily to water, which perhaps was why I liked him so much. To know the ocean, I have always felt, is to recognize the teeth it keeps half-hidden. There was a particular story from Heyerdahl's various writings that I returned to often, reading aloud to myself on nights when sleep was elusive. It was an account of a night on the ocean during one of Heyerdahl's many long overseas expeditions; I had read it first at the age of nine and kept it folded tight in some tidy part of my mind ever after.

As we sank, I tried to recall this story, though as I did so I felt the strangeness of attempting to soothe myself with the very element currently building to unsurvivable pressure over my head.

Chiefly at night, so the story went, *but occasionally in broad daylight, a shoal of small squids shot out of the water precisely like flying fish, gliding through the air as much as up to six feet above the surface, until they lost the speed accumulated below water, and fell down helplessly. In their gliding flight with flaps out they were so much like small flying fish at a distance that we had no idea we saw anything unusual until a live squid flew right into one of the crew and fell down on deck.*

I loved this story. Loved it, I suppose, for its slapstick, but also for the way it went on to suggest that deep things routinely rose to the surface and sometimes even higher than that. In this account, Heyerdahl goes on to describe dark nights on which strange, phosphorescent beings, on some occasions bigger than his craft, reeled up toward the ceiling of the sea and bumped heads before descending. As we sank, I tried to tell myself this story and it worked, to a certain extent—I thought of the way deep things move upward, of the ocean's escapability, even despite its depths. *If you've got breath enough to scream,* as my father said, *you're not drowning,* and so I held my breath and thought about screaming and imagined the ocean coming to an end.

MIRI

I stand beneath the spray of the shower and scream for twenty minutes. I'm all right, for the most part. It is only on occasion that I feel the need to scald myself down to the marrow, sugar-scrub my thighs until I bleed in streaks, and clog the drain with the expendable parts of me. I have spent the morning on the phone, shuttlecocking back and forth between recorded voices, the majority of whom desire a number I cannot provide and the rest of whom want me to know that my call is important. Around noon, I moved the phone from my ear and smashed it some seventeen times into the wall before dropping the remnants and going to fetch a dustpan. Leah had been sitting on the sofa but looked up at this outburst. For a moment, I imagined a kind of reemergence, Leah as I knew her stepping out from behind the baffle of this person and asking me what the fuck I had done. This didn't happen, so after I had cleaned away the pieces of the telephone, I told her I was going to take a shower and that after that I would see about getting a replacement.

I want to explain her in a way that would make you love her, but the problem with this is that loving is something we all do alone and through different sets of eyes. It's nearly impossible, at least in my experience, to listen to someone telling a story about their partner and not wish they'd get to the point a little faster: *OK, so, you're saying he likes long walks, you're saying she's a Capricorn, skip to the end.* It's easy to understand why someone might love a person but far more difficult to push yourself down into that understanding, to pull it up to your chin like bedclothes and feel it settling around you as something true.

The thing about Leah as I knew her was that every so often when I was pissed off and sitting on the sofa, she would grab my legs and start to pedal them, chanting *tour de France tour de France* until I laughed. The thing about Leah was that nine times out of ten she couldn't bring herself to be unkind about anyone, but then three times a year she would say something so blisteringly cruel about someone we knew that she'd clap both hands to her mouth and turn in a circle as though warding off evil. At a point perhaps six months after we'd first started seeing each other, she read a book in which a pair of lesbians emailed each other meaningful lines of poetry and shortly afterward she asked if this was the sort of thing we should be doing, too. *If you ever send me poetry,* I texted her, *I'll cut your tits off,* and over the course of the next week and a half she emailed me every poem from *The Complete Works of Wilfred Owen,* signing off every email with a winking face and a heart.

She told me once that when she was young she would imagine herself with scales that grew beneath the membranes of her skin—a flaking layer of silver-blue between her bones and the surface of her body that would prevent her from becoming waterlogged if she were ever to drown. I used to think of her like this, before we fucked or when she rolled over toward me in the night; about hands pulling her down beneath black water, about scales growing over her eyes.

She taught me to swim because I couldn't, held on to my waist and buoyed me along. *If I wanted to teach you the way I was taught*, she was always saying, *I'd hold you under.* We'd go to the lido in the mornings and sit in the café afterward, damp in our clothes and eating bacon sandwiches and Leah fishing ice out of her Diet Coke.

She invited me to a dinner party with her friends from university: a guy called Toby who lived in a basement flat masquerading as a flat-pack furniture emporium with his much more attractive girlfriend, Sam; a couple of lesbian marine biologists called Allegra and Jess who weren't a couple but had been at some storied prior time; a benignly boring guy called Dan and his loudly bisexual girlfriend, Poppy, who had backcombed her hair like a televangelist and seemed to leave lipstick marks on literally anything that came within a yard of her mouth. I remember that night the way one remembers pivotal things, although in truth nothing earth-shattering happened. I found I liked Toby and Sam far more than I had expected to; they told jokes that weren't at one another's expense, did a *Who's Afraid of Virginia Woolf?* bit that mostly involved slopping wine about and insulting each other before bursting out laughing. *Haven't I got a bitch of a husband*, Sam asked me, winking, vamping up her voice like Liz Taylor. I remember someone put on "Edge of Seventeen" and Toby danced around the kitchen with Jess, mouthing along to the words. Someone had brought Lillet and Jess made Vespers in an assortment of plastic tumblers. There was a vegetarian lasagna, pork chops, and a bowl of mushrooms cooked in port, none of which went together. At one point, Allegra leaned across the table toward me and asked if I didn't think Leah looked exactly like Jean Seberg in *Breathless.* They'd studied on the same course at university and apparently this resemblance was something that all of their classmates had noted. I looked at Leah, currently ferrying cutlery over from the counter—Leah with her short hair and her swimmer's body, the way she moved about the kitchen. *I don't know who Jean Seberg is,* I thought of saying, instead nodding my head and saying, *Yes she does actually, wow I'd never thought of that before.* Someone upset a glass, which spilled its contents before shattering across the kitchen floor, and I was relieved it hadn't been me. *I like the idea of living in the city,* Jess said, *but I think it's just because I hate the idea of being anywhere where I can't immediately locate any other gay people.* Sam opened a bottle of red wine from the co-op and someone asked if there was anything for dessert. *If you say pavlova I'm going to fucking kill myself,* Dan said—actually the only thing I remember him saying all night—*I don't know why people think pavlova is an acceptable thing to serve just because you're having a dinner party.* Across the table, Leah winked at me, and I thought in an unwonted flash that I utterly adored her. *What's wrong with pavlova?* Toby asked, looking hurt. Someone put on an Ella Fitzgerald compilation. *Have you not been with a woman before,* Poppy said to me at one point, red-wine mouthed and leaning toward me with the affect of someone who might have designs on my tonsils. *Have you?* I asked and she burst out laughing. *Oh honey, you know how people are like "I'm gay for Jennifer Aniston, I'm gay for Gillian Anderson," well I'm straight for Dan.*

At the end of the night, Allegra came toward me, bearing down in a gesture I couldn't immediately read and which made me lean back in my chair a little farther than I'd intended. *I haven't come to embrace you,* she said, *you're just sitting on my jacket.* I turned red and fished the jacket out from under me, handed it over without managing to find something intelligent to say.

You'll have to come back, Sam said, hugging me tight and whispering something that I think was intended to be conspiratorial but, since she was rather drunk, was unfortunately only incoherent. Walking to the bus stop together, I told Leah what Poppy had said and she snorted, leaning into my side with a force that knocked me off-balance and which I found I rather enjoyed. *Oh yeah*, she said, grabbing my hand and dragging me into a run as the bus rounded the corner, *Poppy's all right, she just likes people to* know.

"I still don't understand," Carmen says, "why you need a landline."

We're waiting in line at Argos and I can't be bothered to explain to her that I don't need a landline at all, I just need an excuse to be out of the flat.

"It came with the place," I tell her, "you know how it goes. You break it, you bought it."

"*Euripides Eumenides*," she replies, and then says it again when I pretend not to hear her. Carmen read Classical Civilization when we were at university and is at constant pains to remind everyone of this, despite the fact that when pressed she could tell you very little, these days, of what it was she actually studied. Like everyone, most of Carmen's higher education seems to have leaked out of her around her mid-to-late twenties, replaced in the main by methods of treating black mold, by passwords and roast chicken recipes and the symptoms of cervical cancer and thrush.

Once we've bought a new phone, we walk down toward the canal and Carmen has to stop several times to rattle a stone around in the toe of her shoe. *Why don't you take the shoe off,*

I want to say to her, *and take the stone out*, but my head feels sickish and heavy with the promise of oncoming weather, and anyway what difference would it make.

"When I broke up with Tom," Carmen says, "it was hard because for so long afterward I felt like I was still *in it*, d'you know what I mean? Like he'd moved on and I was still in this relationship all by myself."

"When you broke up with Tom," I say, "you threw all his clothes out onto the street." Carmen looks at me like this is hardly the point.

"What I'm saying is, the pain is in the aftermath, more than it is the break."

"Well, we haven't broken up," I say. "But thank you."

Carmen is wearing her glasses today and they give her eyes a near-telescopic exaggeration. We walk along the towpath sandwiched between the canal and the fenced-off gardens of the houses that back onto the water and she asks me what it is I'm worrying about.

"She's been away so often before," she says to me without waiting for an answer but in the kind of voice that strains to make it clear she's open to unpleasant confidences. "Even before this time, I mean. I know it's for her job or whatever but I can imagine it's frustrating. It's difficult to navigate a relationship like that—everything always working to her schedule. Especially this time, with how long it took, with how long it was *supposed* to take. The world doesn't revolve around her, around when she decides to be home, you know?"

OK, I think of saying, *but that's not the point. The problem isn't that she went away, it's that nothing about her going away felt normal. It isn't that her being back is difficult, it's that I'm not convinced she's really back at all.*

Of course, I haven't actually given Carmen many details, which does make things harder to explain. Carmen might know that Leah was only supposed to be away for three weeks but she doesn't know how Leah has been behaving, for the most part, I think, because I'm too exhausted by the prospect of her comparing it to something that Tom used to do. *I remember when I was with Tom and he'd play* Red Dead Redemption *all day and eat Pringles and not put his shoes away, so believe me I know what you're going through.* This, I suppose, is unfair of me. Carmen's my friend—my best friend, I sometimes worry—and I'm supposed to want to share my miseries with her, to grasp her hand and confide all the blandly conventional problems that pepper my day as much as anybody else's. I do love her, I think for her familiarity, for the way she demands to see me where other old friendships have fallen by the wayside, the victims of mutual inattention. She is a good friend, inasmuch as she is a present friend, or at least a friend who likes to make plans. And yet too often I find myself stoppered by unwillingness to admit to basic frustrations, to look at her across a coffee shop table and respond to her humdrum admissions with a straight *me, too.* Carmen talks about her bad dates, about arguing with her brothers, about hating her next-door neighbors for always allowing their children to kick balls against the dividing wall, and I listen and I nod and I give her advice and I tell her things are fine with me, that I really can't complain. I suppose, in the main, this comes from a wish to appear in control, if not to say superior. I hate and have always hated her insistence on comparing Tom to Leah, and perhaps I have allowed this feeling to bleed too freely into everything else, allowed myself to clam up around the possibility of shared experience. Really, no one should feel as paralyzingly

superior as I do around Carmen, around a lot of people, especially given that in many ways I have little enough to back this
feeling up. It's a failing, and one I am aware of. Carmen is patient with me, I think, or perhaps she simply doesn't recognize
my behavior as rudeness, accepts my role as a good listener as
synonymous with being a good friend. Leah always used to
say that I was kind, but I've never felt at all convinced of that.
You're interested in people, she would say, *you like to hear about
their siblings,* and I would tell her I wasn't sure that was the
same as being kind to them.

"Miri?"

I realize I have not spoken in several minutes and Carmen
is looking at me with a keenness that is at least 40 percent real,
though unquestionably assisted by the magnification of her
eyes behind her glasses.

"It's all OK," I say vaguely, hoping this answers whatever
question it is I have been asked, "I'm just tired, you know?"

This, at least, is something true, something I feel I can give
to her. Over the past few weeks, exhaustion has settled in the
arches of my feet, in the small of my back.

"I hear you," Carmen says, reaching out to touch my arm
and then changing the subject to some issue she's been having
in getting her passport renewed. The day has turned suddenly
nauseating—smell of sulfur from a backed-up drain—and I
look toward the canal and wish this city were not veined with
water like the lines on the back of a hand.

LEAH

I remember when I was twelve and I first read about the Challenger Deep. This is—or was, at one point—the deepest known point of the ocean, located in the Western Pacific at one end of the Mariana Trench. In 1960, a Swiss-designed submersible craft, the *Trieste*, was piloted down to this point—a record at the time—by the Swiss oceanographer Jacques Piccard and an American naval officer named Don Walsh. The descent, which took almost five hours, resulted in a grand total of twenty minutes spent on the ocean floor before the two men decided to take the craft back up again. According to reports, they would have spent longer down there, but the outer window of their vessel had started to crack on descent.

I read about this in one of my father's books, the name of which I no longer recall, though I remember its turquoise cover and the illustrated submarine casting its exterior lights onto the title in an eerie downward spill. I must have taken that book down from my father's shelf more times than he considered strictly polite, because at one point I pulled it out and found he had printed his name on the inside cover: *Property of Michael Henry Frayne, on long lease to his daughter Leah.* There was something I loved, aged twelve, about the way the book spoke so coolly of the deep ocean, not as something to be survived or conquered but simply navigated. It made me think about the straight imperative of technology, the way anything could be constructed to solve a problem. Coffee makers make coffee, trains carry you places in a hurry, and submarines allow you to travel farther than the ocean's vastness and your ill-equipped body should permit. I suppose the book spoke to the part of my imagination that still held on to the thought of the sea as something unknowable—spoke to and, in a sense, calmed it. I don't know that my endless reading and rereading of the book was what specifically instilled in me the desire to explore the ocean. More likely, I simply read it so much that it fell apart and I had to go and find something else to do, like exploring the ocean.

––––––––

I said to myself, OK that's enough, *and then said it again* aloud to ensure I meant it. I told Jelka to stay where she was and took Matteo through to the rear chamber to assess the situation. There was little enough to be gained from doing this—Matteo had already checked every piece of equipment that could be checked and found them in fine working order—but taking a moment away from Jelka's incessant humming was frankly result enough. The rear chamber was narrow and arranged like a small galley kitchen-cum-study. There were lockers along the back wall and a table with bench seating, a small sink and sideboard for food preparation, a bookshelf and a table for taking notes, a storage box shaped like a chest freezer, two foldout bunks arranged one on top of the other across one wall. The craft was one of the smallest I had ever been on, resembling nothing so much as an upside-down light bulb, designed to drop like a stone. At the base, the control deck, rear chamber, and wash stall were sealed off from the rest of the craft in a pressurized hull, the only doors the ones between the deck, chamber, and stall and the lower hatch leading to the escape trunk.

I looked around for a moment, as if assessing for damage. Matteo shone a torch into the corners.

"I'd like a rare steak," he said, apropos of nothing. "I'd like a rare steak and a drink." I looked at him, registering again the curious sensation of blandness, *yes well*ness. We were still falling, had no way of stopping, and I felt very little about this beyond a mild sense of incorrectness, a soft constriction at the back of my neck, like someone had taken hold of the flesh and pinched. I watched as Matteo made his way around the lockers, squinting into the white shaft of the torchlight, as if expecting something dreadful to emerge. He had only three fingers on his left hand and held the torch somewhat awkwardly in his right, with which he was still less dominant. He had told me the story once, long ago, before we both came to work for the Centre. We were working on a midsize submersible some-where in the Arctic Basin, Matteo as the chief engineer and I as part of a small team of biologists conducting species invento-ries and studying certain proteins present in the bloodstreams of cold-water fish. One night, Matteo had held his fingers out before him like a TV medium and told me how, when he was a teenager, he'd gone ice fishing with his father at Lake Simcoe, not far from the Durham Region of Southern Ontario. It was a four-day drive from San Luis Obispo, California, where he had scrawled out a broadly uninterrupted childhood existence of spray-can cheese and TV and bed when his mother said so, but as his father told him on the morning of their departure: *nothing worth seeing is ever only walking distance away.* This was baseless California logic at best, but Matteo still took it to heart—*my dad*, he once said, *loved a slogan and I bought whatever he sold*. It was during this fishing trip that Matteo developed such bad frostbite that he lost significant movement and ultimately all but the cigarette fingers and thumb on his left held. I had looked at his nails, lumpy as oyster shells, black around the cuticles. I had asked him what his father had done when he'd realized what was happening, and Matteo had shaken his head at me, explained that he hadn't told him. *End of the third day, when I realized the skin of my hand was changing color, I just put my gloves on and used my right hand to hold the fishhook for the rest of the trip. It felt too important, you know? I didn't want to ruin it. I didn't want to go just yet.*

We stood in the rear chamber for a long time, just looking around, unsure of what it was we were hoping to see. After a while, I registered a vague rumbling, a gentle sense of alteration in the floor beneath me, which I couldn't identify until Matteo pointed out that we were slowing down.

MIRI

I typically think it's easiest to feel warm when a part of us is cold. I lie in bed with my feet uncovered and try to feel this, chase a sensation of something up my leg and lose it. It's getting on for autumn and Leah has been back nearly two months—thin colorless light in the morning and spiders all over the house. The neighbors play American football on the television at odd hours and Leah runs the taps and I think about my mother more than is usual.

The morning before her funeral, I'd taken six Nurofen together with a spill of cooking brandy and the combination of the two had set off a curious Doppler effect whereby sensations seemed to strike me out of order: the smell of food before I tasted it, the feeling of my glass in my hand long after the realization that I'd dropped it. The reception was held at my aunt's, as my mother's house was too far out to be practical, not to mention in partial disrepair. I remember very little of the event, though I know that at one point Leah took me outside onto the back porch and told me we ought to stay there a while. *I'm sorry,* I remember saying, although in response to what I'm not sure, *sometimes I just say these things. I don't really know why.* I remember standing where I was and the light hitting me in pieces, first my face and then the back of my hands, my chest, the underside of my jaw. I remember the cold, and looking down into my aunt's garden and then across a banked slate wall into the garden beyond, where a man was burning waste with a can of kerosene held at shoulder height. I remember staring down into the smoke, an odd, druidic thing, flames stark in the white afternoon. The man had piled leaves and cardboard boxes, barrels rotted out and green with mildew—a thick-bodied bulk of a bonfire, tapering up into a spindle that smoked and spat out ash. It had been easy to imagine, though I knew it wasn't wise, a human form at the center of this conflagration. Quite easy to imagine the corporeal something taking shape among the ashes—barrels blurring into rounded shoulders, the toothless brooms and buckets shucking off their clarity and re-forming as the possibilities of necks and heads and melting human faces. *I want to go inside now*, I remember saying to Leah but she shook her head and said we could go around the front of the house and stand there for a while, if the bonfire smell was bothering me.

Having fitted the new phone, I have no choice but to use it. I program the Centre into the handset's automated dial function, so that now I only have to key in a single digit to kick-start the day. In the mornings, I slice thin-skinned Meyer lemons into water and pretend a breakfast for Leah from only this, place the glass on a tray and hope the offering doesn't come across as sarcastic. Cold water with lemon is one of the few things I have found she will reliably drink, though occasionally I have caught her spooning table salt into the mixture and have taken the glass away. When she eats anything at all, she eats salted things, which makes me worry, appears to crave olives and anchovies, licks the blood that seeps from her gums in the early mornings. Some days, I imagine her lunatic on salt water, vainly try to slip oranges into her diet, crush raspberries with the flat of a knife and imagine sneaking them into her tooth-paste. When I was a child, my mother taught me about scurvy, and ever since I have pictured it leering out at me with the prevalence of the common cold. I picture Leah's symptoms, convince myself that her bleedings and sheddings might all be put down to a simple lack of vitamin C. *Early symptoms*, I read from my phone screen, hidden under the covers like a teen-ager texting a crush, *include weakness and tiredness, sore hands, arms, and legs. Without treatment, decreased red blood cells, gum disease, changes to hair, and bleeding from the skin may occur.* I look at Leah and try to imagine the conversation: me leaning across the table to tell her, *Darling, I think you have scurvy*, and Leah nodding her head, looking up and saying, *Yes I think I do, thank goodness you pointed it out.*

I am falling behind on my work, find it difficult to sit with-out sweating, without standing up again, convinced there is something on my chair. Overtired, sweat crescents yellowing the underarms of shirts. My inbox is scrambled over with in-quiries, clients scuttling to express their displeasure as fast as they can recognize a crisis. *Please send reassurance that you have started work on the grant proposal*, one client has started messag-ing upward of three times a day. I eat canned ravioli and try to remember what it meant to be concerned about an unpleasant tone in an email. Somewhere in the flat, Leah is running the taps again.

We have a fight about this, several mornings later; Leah sit-ting at the kitchen table and looking at the toast I've set before her, at the orange I've placed beside it, at the kiwi fruit and raspberry jam.

"No, I don't want this," she says, and so I tell her I don't want to pay my half of the water bill this month, and we go on from there. She behaves like a houseguest, I tell her, like a person who's blown into my home and sat down like she belongs. She says she doesn't know what to say to me. *Say anything*, I want to scream, *say I knew what I signed up for when you went away, say you told me the deal, that you gave me all the information. Say it was my choice, to be OK with it, that it's not your fault you went away for so long. Say it was my choice to move into the spare room. Say it's my choice to come into the bathroom every morning when I know what it is that I'll find.*

"I don't think," I say instead, "that you're eating the right things."

"Is that it," she says to me, then abruptly takes up the orange and throws it against the wall. It hits the brickwork with the wet cottony sound of an internal organ. I watch the orange roll across the floor and think about laughing, picture some soft internal part of Leah skittling over the kitchen tiles and vanishing beneath the fridge.

———

Leah worked at the aquarium as a teenager. It was the sort of dirty-glamorous history I loved about her, an image I wanted to roll around in—my Leah with her shag-cut hair at seventeen, feeding dolphins in a wet suit cut off at the knees. I never knew her at this age, of course, though I've seen pictures. She showed me a sleeve of them once, early on, passing a hand over her face when I laughed at her dyed-black hair, her nose ring, and her overtweezed eyebrows. *I was just trying something*, she said, *my mum hated the hair dye so I did it even though it looked terrible, you know.* In one photograph, a teenaged Leah crouches by a tall, cylindrical tank containing what she identified to me as a giant Pacific octopus named Pamela. *We were pals*, she said, in a voice that I thought seemed to strive for offhandedness. *Did you know they taste with their skin? Octopuses, I mean.* In the old days, I used to enjoy this, Leah's seemingly never-ending list of useless facts, acquired from a teenagerhood spent changing the water in clownfish tanks and encouraging children to handle spiny creatures in the touch pools. She told me a story once that I often thought about afterward, replayed for myself like a favorite movie. Leah, aged eighteen: letting a girlfriend into the aquarium one night after-hours, sharing vodka shaken up with supermarket lemonade and kissing on the floor beside the Open Ocean tank in view of reeling schools of yellowfin tuna, of sardines and moon jellies and stingrays, of copper rockfish and hammerhead sharks. She had, so the story went, stuck intrepid hands down the girl's bootcut jeans and afterward taken her into the octopus room to meet Pamela, though on doing so she had found the creature had died in her tank sometime in the late afternoon.

When I returned to this story later, I would superimpose an eighteen-year-old me over the top of the girlfriend, scribbling her out and sketching my lines in more permanent ink. In this edited version, we would kiss—eighteen-year-old Leah and me—and then afterward she'd take me to the octopus room, rap her fingertips on the glass cylinder, and Pamela wouldn't be dead. She would rise up out of some corner and shiver toward us, pulsing flex of a parasol opening and closing, the mantle and suckers and the head like something primed to burst. She would feel her way across the side of the tank and in this scene (or dream, or version) I would know, because of my astonishing ability to know such things, that she had intended to meet me, that for any other girlfriend she would have died but that for me she had waited. I would splay my hand against the glass and imagine I felt the great gelatinous give of her body, the folds and spongy inner membranes, the secret place where her three hearts beat out blueish copper blood. All quite fantastical, of course. By the time I was eighteen, Pamela was dead and I had yet to kiss a girl.

I got so depressed when she died, Leah told me once. It wasn't really my job to look after her, you know, I was just a volunteer, but sometimes when the senior staff were feeding her they'd let me touch her. They'd open the top of the tank and she'd sort of boil up toward you, all these arms wrapping up around yours, all these suckers, and then she'd just sort of hold you there, look at you. She didn't try to pull me into the water, exactly, but it could be difficult to get her to detach until she was ready. She'd hold me there, my chest up against the edge of the tank, sort of bent over and staring down at her. And then she'd let me go. They said she liked me—I don't know if that was true, but it was nice.

Leah had long been a martyr to gifts that centered octopuses in some fashion. The same way that anyone who makes the mistake of committing to an animal will receive chicken- or elephant- or dolphin-themed gifts every birthday and Christmas for the rest of their lives, so Leah was constantly writing notes to thank people for octopus jewelry and octopus trinket dishes and cake forks with octopus handles that were semi-impossible to hold. I had, for the most part, made a point of avoiding this trope, except once, on Leah's thirtieth birthday, when I gave her a sleeve of promotional postcards from the aquarium at which she'd once worked. It was something I'd found quite by chance, on an eBay listing, a book of branded cards, at least fifteen years old, each labeled THE STARS OF OUR SHOW and showing images ranging from the aquarium's single giant sea turtle to the otter tank and the dolphins and the penguin exhibit. The last card but one showed a tangerine-colored octopus, its left eye swiveled toward the camera, its tentacles thrown up above its head, as though tumbling downward through air, rather than water. The printed label at the bottom left-hand corner of the card read: PAMELA—GIANT PACIFIC OCTOPUS—ESTIMATED AGE BETWEEN 3 AND 4 YEARS OLD. I had given the cards to Leah and she had cried about them and kissed me, and I'm really only telling this story now because it makes me look good, and because Leah always took the postcard of Pamela with her on work trips after that.

When we met, Leah was working in research and conservation for a facility that specialized in the protection of coastal and deep-sea ecosystems. This was before the Centre—long before it even existed, in fact, which often surprises people. I think it has something to do with the name, the Centre for Marine Enquiry, a blandness that implies longevity, a patrician sense of having always been there, of being a long-established institution, which of course it is not. As it was, Leah didn't move to the Centre until many years after we met, having worked the full span of her twenties for the same small operation. On an early date, she poured olive oil, dipped bread, told me a story about a company she'd once hoped to work for that specialized in applying the physical adaptations of underwater species to industrial innovation. They had engineered a new type of door handle that mimicked the structure of sharkskin and made it more difficult for germs and viruses to attach. *Sharkskin is basically made up of millions of tiny teeth*, she said, pouring wine, talking with her mouth full. *They're called "dermal denticles," isn't that great? Practically speaking, a shark's skin is almost as likely to do you damage as its mouth is. It didn't really end up being my area—I'm more straight biology—but*

I still love the idea of finding a way to harness odd little things like that to do some kind of service. We ate Russian beef stew with dill and talked the way people do on early dates, extravagantly confessional, every statement an attempt at some self-defining truth: *I'm the type of person who cries at movies, I'm the type of person who works better alone.* After the restaurant, we drank Dark and Stormys at a bar unfamiliar to either of us, talked about favorite meals and favorite places. The night was wet, air close and flannel-damp, reports of ball lightning hitting the power lines some half a mile from my home. *I'm a Catholic,* I said at one point, *so I believe in punishment but not reward.* When we kissed—first kiss, wet-palmed, tongues stickled with ginger—I thought about sharkskin and pushed my hand into the space where Leah's shirt had pulled free from her waistband. The next morning, I woke too early, my bedroom window filled with sharp segments of light.

———

I'm not sure what the sound is at first, and then I am sure, and then it is Leah screaming. It is a Wednesday, or possibly a Thursday, and I am not awake except in the parts of me required to jackknife out of bed. The scream seems wrong at first, garbled up into something other. It takes me several moments to recognize this interference as Leah's sound machine—her screams half-drowned by the swelling, the oozing, the sinking noise, like a mouth forced open and leaking something thick. It's dark, and I can't find the light switch, and the noise is louder in the corridor, louder still toward the barrier of Leah's bedroom door. I reflect, in some faraway part of myself, that every horror movie begins like this: no lights and a voice in the darkness, feet tangled in bedclothes, a knocking hand left aloft as the door swings back. I push the door, take in the room that used to belong to both of us. Leah is there, and the bed is soaking, and it takes me longer than it should, even in darkness, to realize the water is coming from her. As I stand in the doorway, she screams and keeps on screaming, apparently unaware of my presence, and the sound is only interrupted when her body contorts, convulses, and she vomits a shower of water across the bed. I'm not sure what happens after this, only that the screaming proves to have been almost entirely unconscious, as when I shake her awake it stops and she stares at me, mouth swollen with salt, and she doesn't seem to know me at all.

Midnight Zone

LEAH

Sea floor, full dark. About half an hour after the craft came to its miraculously gentle stop, Matteo started vainly trying to send distress signals again, though as Jelka pointed out there was little to no sense in doing this, since we were onboard the only vessel capable of diving to such a depth.

"What are they going to do," she said, her impulse to pray apparently cut short by irritation, "send a search party ten thousand feet then throw a rope ladder the rest of the way?" I remember her then, glaring at us, as thin as I have ever known a person to be and still be able to move around.

None of us commented on the strangeness of the situation, on the way a routine research dive had so quickly turned into this. As before, during the fall, the impulse to question felt curiously flattened, the notion of how this had happened somehow beside the point. I smelled burning flesh again, just for a moment, and thought about saying something, then distracted myself with thoughts of things I had left above sea level, of polystyrene cups and orange juice and pizza, of the sound of our neighbors' television and the way Miri bit at the skin of her lip so often that kissing tasted bloody; metallic zip of a licked battery. *Sunken thoughts*, I imagined her saying, and turned my face toward the windows. Without lights, the water was blind around us and holding torches to the glass resulted in little but our own faces reflected back—ghost forms in deep water, six eyes peering in from without.

There are five main layers to the ocean, at least if you go by scientific designation. The first is the Epipelagic, or Sunlight Zone (also known as the Photic Zone), which covers the distance between the surface and approximately six hundred feet beneath. Here, there is only minimal pressure, coral reefs, color, and pleasure divers, the option to hold your breath and jump. After that comes the Mesopelagic, or Twilight Zone, reaching an approximate three thousand feet, at which point sunlight may still penetrate, though beyond this drop comes the Bathypelagic, or Midnight Zone, and from here on, you're down in the dark. At around thirteen thousand feet and below, you pass through the Abyssopelagic, or Abyssal Zone, an area whose name roughly translates to "no bottom." No light here, of course, and temperatures a little above freezing, though you will still encounter life, of a fashion, at this depth. Things come down this far and farther, though they seldom come with blood and bones included. Once you reach depths of thirteen thousand feet, everything has a strange name but rarely a backbone: vampire squid and zombie worms, cosmic jellyfish, tripodfish and faceless cusks and pelican eels. Creatures that live this deep are frequently solitary and only infrequently seen. There are big things down here, old things, and certainly more of them than we know about. Almost every piloted dive to these depths has uncovered something new.

Beyond this point, there is a final layer, though the farthest depths of the sea are fragmented and interspersed among trenches formed by tectonic subduction, where the plates of Earth converge and the older, denser plate is pushed down beneath the lighter, creating fissures and places for things to drop deep. This layer is known as the Hadalpelagic, or Hadal Zone, a name that speaks for itself. Lying between roughly nineteen and thirty-six thousand feet, much of this layer of the water is unexplored, which is not to say uninhabited. It was difficult to tell exactly how far we had fallen without the system online to give us a read. It would, I suppose, have been entirely possible to hit the seabed without falling into one of the trenches, although looking out onto the blackness, I believed almost without question that we had fallen as far as it was possible to go. It was difficult to imagine anywhere deeper than the place we had ended up.

MIRI

Leah and my mother never met for a number of reasons, most conveniently because by the time Leah and I were serious enough for the issue to arise, my mother was already quite ill. Leah was good about this, for the most part; rarely asked and didn't seem to take offense. When I visited my mother at her house, before I moved her, I often came away afraid of insane things, spent days afterward terrified of the ceilings falling, of being bitten, of something crawling up my leg—and Leah was patient with this the way I ultimately came to see as central to the whole of her. In the nights directly following my visits, I would fall asleep in often unexplainable panic and Leah would soothe me, tell me she had me, press her hands into the small of my back. She discovered it was easy to calm me down by repeating words whose shapes I found appealing, muttered *redolent* and *pelt* and *chicanery* until I fell asleep.

On occasion, and typically out of nowhere, I would wonder whether this level of patience would hold out, should a test ever prove I was likely to develop the same condition as my mother. On occasion, I would look in the mirror and consider the briskly diminishing fact of myself, hold my hands to the sides of my face as if preventing collapse. *Would you look after me*, I found myself wanting to ask and unable to do so, the request tangling back on itself, coming out as *would you pass the gravy, would you change the channel, would you look at this.* For a long time, it failed to occur to me that I was not, in fact, the only person this could happen to. I would look into the mirror and imagine that only I could be in any sense finite.

———

I don't realize until well after the fact that I haven't been expecting to get through to anyone actually able to help me. The phone calls to the Centre have simply established themselves as routine, akin to hair brushing, to running my finger across my teeth and calling them clean. The morning it works, I am already planning the rest of my day: idle pileup of tea and spoons and gummy vitamins, unread emails and post left unopened and linens changed, salt hidden, residue scrubbed from the sides of the bath. At the table: two plates, the crusts of bread rolls with their insides picked out, a pitcher of day-old water growing a skin. We haven't spoken about the previous night, though the bed in which Leah sleeps has dried and her behavior seems largely unaffected. I have googled and found the results mostly unhelpful: *reasons for vomiting clear liquid—do you have acute gastroenteritis? Have you drunk too much water? Have you been making yourself sick?*

Leah is locked in the bathroom, humming something that might be a song I recognize but almost certainly isn't. I am listening to the sound of the taps, to the sound of her humming, and thinking for whatever reason of the clutter of my mother's bathroom shelves: the cold cream and Jungle Formula and the Blue Grass perfume that she always kept in its box with the turquoise and cream Celtic lettering. The space around us is a claw half-grasped, holding tight without quite crushing, and I wish, in the idle way I always wish it these days, that I felt more confident in my ability to breathe.

I am staring out of the window when the hold music cuts

midchorus and a voice comes online, asking me in businesslike fashion how it is they can help me today. Automatically, I start to recite the numbers—rank number, transfer number, and so on, and so on—but the voice interrupts to assure me they already have all the details they need.

"I'm sorry if it's been a bit of a process," the voice adds, in a tone that could convey almost any emotion, "getting in touch with us."

The upstairs neighbors are playing a soap opera on the television, a woman screaming in a voice that tries and fails to convince that this isn't what she'd wanted at all.

———————

I remember a time that Leah went away. Not the *time, but* a point long before she was working for the Centre, a point at which expeditions were still infrequent—brief dives off the coast of Scotland, weeks abroad on fishing trawlers, research trips to places I could find on a map. The way I remember it is this: late September, washed-down dregs of a liquid summer. The seasons always change more swiftly on the water, the light on the sea autumnal long before the chill has reached the city, and I was far from the city that day, having traveled miles to see Leah off. The afternoon they left, I watched from the viewing deck along with three or four of the other wives, one of whom complained of being cold until a staffer from the rig offered her a life jacket in a bid to shut her up. *Colder on the water*, she said, over and over again, *should have thought of that, should have brought something warmer.*

I remember the slip of the craft across the water, long metal nose and sculpted conning tower, the way it seemed to dip and slink, eel-like, white lights along its spine and finial.

I watched it float, not bobbing, seeming less to sit upon the water than to hang within it, half-submerged and threatening to sink. I remember turning to the woman on my right and saying I wasn't sure a ship like that could possibly withstand the ocean's weight on top of it, that the crew would all be crushed, that we ought to speak to someone. This woman, I forget whose wife she was, only smiled at me, took my hand, and said that first timer always felt like this. *You expect them to come back looking like Flat Stanley*, she said, and I told her I wasn't a first timer and asked her who Flat Stanley was and she asked if I'd really never read those books and in the ensuing conversation I moved my eyes away from the water long enough to miss the ship going down. By the time I looked back there was nothing—bob of gulls upon an undisturbed surface, gentle sense of something pooling in my wrists as if my heart had momentarily stopped.

Now the thing is, from everything I know and everything I have otherwise experienced, it seems unlikely that the ship could have gone down that quickly, and certainly not with such minimal disturbance on the top. But even so, this is what I remember and short of getting in contact with the other wives onboard the viewing deck that day, none of whose names I even recall, there is no way of checking this scenario for accuracy. What I remember, then, becomes what happened: Leah leaving like the summer from the ocean, not by degrees but all at once.

The last time she went away was different—for one thing, I wasn't there. After the Centre threw their going-away party, I went home and Leah didn't and that night I dreamed auroral

colors and woke at three to a white rubbernecking moon at
the window, which I chose not to find unsettling.

Three weeks is not a long time. One can wait three weeks
for a parcel and think very little of it. For a while, I tightroped
a careful normality, considered calling friends and asking them
to entertain me, did my work and listened to the neighbors'
television and broadly speaking didn't think of much at all.

When three weeks had passed and Leah did not return, the
Centre called to tell me there had been a delay. *How exactly
can a submarine be delayed?* I asked—imagined underwater toll
roads, found myself on the precipice of a laugh. It was nothing, so they said, to be concerned about. Provisionally, the vessel was stocked for several months, the oxygen would continue
to replenish. *But it won't be several months, will it?* The voice on
the end of the line assured me it would not.

I went to the movies alone on a Tuesday lunchtime, lined
my wallet with contraband sweets, which I ate in the dark,
unscrewing each from its polythene wrap with a noise that
would have been thrillingly antisocial had there been anyone
there to annoy. Afterward, I moved through the city the way
one might in bad weather, though the day was clear and my
head bent down against nothing. There was, as of course I
now know, something terribly wrong already, but I question
how much I really understood then, what significance I can attach to a bad day, to an upset stomach. In general, I was unsure
of how to behave. The Centre called again to tell me there was
nothing to worry about and I tried to ask questions but found
it difficult to argue with the brightness of the voice on the line.
OK thank you, I remember I said, somehow unable to summon
the bad manners required to protest against such meaningless
reassurance, *I really am grateful you called.* I was, I remember,

anxious not to offend the person whose updates were broadly unhelpful but who might, I imagined, quite easily stop calling if I said the wrong thing.

At the two-month mark, I wondered briefly about joining a support group for military wives and dismissed this, consulted notice boards in the newsagents but found only choirs and Addicts Anonymous, a phone line for smokers, and a book group for women with GAD. I lifted up flyers that had been pinned in such a way as to obscure older ones, imagined pulling a card from some hidden place and holding it up to the light: WIFE UNDER THE SEA? HERE'S THE NUMBER TO CALL. In the end, I took a flyer advertising cleaning services at a knockdown rate and left the newsagent without buying anything.

---

*This is not to say that I didn't keep busy. I was still work-*ing then, of a fashion, still keeping up with Carmen, whom I apprised only a little of what was going on. I had been alone before, after all; I knew the ways in which time knit together, the hours of television and cans of soup and sleeves of dates it takes to make up a day. Leah's friends would call at irregular intervals—most frequently Toby or Sam, both of whom had become my friends over the intervening years since our first dinner party. We talked fairly often and I filled my days this way, texted Sam about the books she was reading, kept up a string of messages with Toby over the programs playing on the neighbors' television, a topic that never ceased to fascinate him. *Do you think*, he had said to me once, *that they're running some sort of illegal operation up there and the television is just to drown out the noise?* For whatever reason, I was vague about the situation, told Carmen and Sam that Leah was delayed but that it was nothing to worry about, that she'd be back in a month at most. *So OK*, Sam said, *don't you think that you'd like to come eat with us this evening?* I told her I'd love to, really, but that a friend was away for the weekend and I'd promised to look after her cat. After hanging up, I wondered why I'd said this, crossed to the fridge and peered in at the expired tubs of Chinese food, at the net bag of lemons turning black.

In the mornings, I'd go for a run, give up at some halfway point and buy a coffee, walk back with the sweat drying cold on my arms. I was tired, sore-jawed, sore-boned in the evenings. I wrote my grant applications, emailed clients, watched television, bought a cheap pair of boots online. Sometimes, I imagined calling the Centre and didn't. Overall, I don't believe I looked as concerned as I could have done.

This is not an attempt to sound callous. What you have to understand is that, unpleasant or not, all of this had more or less happened before. Trawlers were often delayed and dives were often extended, in the same way that evening trains to the city were canceled by hail or by somebody caught on the tracks. It was all work, with all the usual delay and frustration. More than once, Leah had been held up without explanation, had wound up home belated and weary and smelling of salt. *Sometimes I think you prefer it down there*, I had said to her, holding her face in my hands and wondering whether I meant it to sound like a joke or reproach, *you go so deep you forget you're supposed to come back.*

———

I went to a party held by Leah's friends—Poppy from the long-ago dinner party gesturing in a manner I assumed to be self-deprecating around the generous loft apartment she shared with her boyfriend, Dan. To be honest, I'm not entirely sure why I went. I had never much warmed to Poppy, to her aggressively changeable hairdo and her way of talking over the ends of other people's sentences like the music that plays to keep acceptance speeches short. It's possible, I suppose, that the fact of three months without Leah was working on me harder than I wished to recognize. On occasion, I would crawl under my desk at noon and sleep through my lunch break. I felt more certain than usual that something was off about the color of my tongue. Company, in whatever form, suddenly seemed more appealing than it had done. Prior to leaving the house I had smoothed my fingers across my eyebrows to flatten them and watched the rain of dead skin with some consternation. *How long*, I asked myself, *has it been since I last washed my face?*

The music was loud. A blur of conversation between unfamiliar people and Sam somewhere at my side, poking my hip with a finger to make me move. In the kitchen, Poppy argued with Dan about something to do with the texture of the dip he was making. Sam found a bottle of wine, pinched three plastic cups from a sideboard, and poured one out for each of us, nestling her cup inside the empty third, which she was saving for whenever Toby arrived. I looked at her hands around the two cups and missed Leah, hard—missed the fact of saved spaces, of saying something in unison, of turning to one another afterward as if to say *thank god it was you*. I blinked, found that Sam was saying something to me. *You should drink that*, she repeated, *you look a little white*. I said nothing to this, imagined my mouth was filling with water, wished I could escape to a bathroom and check on the color of my tongue.

Sometime later, Leah's friend Allegra, who had been at that

first dinner party, came over to ask me how I was. She was wearing tennis shoes and a long white sweater and I remember wanting to tell her I liked this outfit and then feeling certain she wouldn't care to know what I thought. She sat beside me on the windowsill and asked me how I was, which no one had exactly done up to this point. I told her it was difficult and she nodded at me, tipped her plastic cup against mine. *I hear you*, she said, and I wondered idly why she and Leah had never dated. *You know you can call me if you need to talk about anything*, she said, *even if you just want to have a whine. It's really shitty, I know.* I thanked her for this, feeling briefly warm in a way I would forget about almost immediately afterward. *That's really nice of you*, I said, and then, *This wine is disgusting.*

When I got home, I found a message from the Centre on my answering machine, suggesting—in a voice that seemed to glance at its watch—that I try not to worry, that it was all going exactly to plan. I played the message over several times, imagining I heard another voice in the background, perhaps instructing the caller on what to say.

———

I started losing time a little. The Centre still called, but a little less frequently. I thought about trying to find them several times around this point, searching futilely through their website for an address or any contact information besides their switchboard. Summer slunk into the brickwork, bloating the building outward, pressure in the walls. The space above the oven swelled and leaked some viscous substance like a body pierced between its ribs. I began to grow delinquent with my emails, sleeping poorly and at badly chosen times of day. *Is this normal?* Sam texted, and I had to think for longer than I care to admit before realizing she meant the length of Leah's absence. *They say it's all standard*, I replied. *Did you know that submarines are able to produce their own indefinite supply of air? The only limitations are the amount of food onboard, or sustaining some sort of major technological defect.* I had looked this information up online some moments earlier and hoped quite keenly that she didn't realize this.

I found an online group for women who liked to role-play that their husbands had gone to space. I'm not entirely sure how this came about, though I believe it was probably a byproduct of my fruitless search for a support group that really spoke to me. I spent several days moving through the message boards, reading conversations between women about their fantasy husbands, learning forum slang, not posting anything. *MHIS* [my husband in space] was a common acronym, as was *BS* [before space], *EB* [earthbound], and *CBW* [came back wrong].

MHIS was such a loving partner, a typical post might run, *a friend and helpmeet, a wonderful father, but ever since he came back things have been different, I wonder if he CBW.*

Six years and counting on MHIS, might run another. *I know us EB wives all have it tough but sometimes I worry I don't have the natural reserves of patience it takes to make it. It can be very hard just to wait for the end of his MTM* [mission to Mars] *without so much as a message to let me know he's safe. Most of the time it's easiest not to think about him at all.*

Beneath each post would run scores of comments: women feeding in with their own fictitious experiences of husbands lost to impossible missions, husbands orbiting the moons of Jupiter, husbands strewn across space. After a while, I started to wonder whether the thrill of the fantasy wasn't so much the thought of their husbands returning as the part where they wished them away.

New here, I typed once, *EB, looking to talk*. I lingered over this message for several minutes but ultimately chose not to post it, finding that none of the acronyms fitted me well enough to bother.

I imagined my mother's symptoms and read them into the way that I swallowed, the way that I shaped my words. I fell prey to patterns of terrible thinking, imagined myself crowded with cysts, with cancer, growing an untreatable skin. I went to the doctor several times, detailing imaginary ailments, and was asked whether there was anything causing me anxiety. *I've always been like this*, I wanted to say, *it's just that she made it better.* The doctor explained that hypochondria's very insidiousness lay in its creeping logic, in the ways it purported to make sense. It's very easy to locate one symptom and then go in search of another, to knit them together in a way that will satisfy almost any diagnosis. If you're experiencing fatigue, vision problems, and tingling hands, the logical conclusion is multiple sclerosis. To a hypochondriac, any other inference smacks of little but refusal to look at the facts. *Try*, the doctor said, *to be a little less logical. Sometimes symptoms just happen, we don't really know why.*

The weather was changing, wet and bulbous and warm. One day, I sat in the window of the bedroom all afternoon and watched the flying ants foam the glass, collecting in the tip of the guttering and overflowing, falling to the gravel drive below. That night, around ten or eleven o'clock, the phone rang but the person on the line refused to speak when I answered. The number that flashed on the phone display looked to be that of the Centre, but no prompting would persuade the caller to speak and after four minutes of silence I once again heard the dial tone. After this, I sat on the floor of the kitchen and thought about Leah, about the shape of her feet and the way she spoke about her father, the special voice she used to talk to cats, her kind frown, her intonation, her fingernails. I thought about the time we kissed at the movies and a guy jerked off behind us and I complained to the management. I thought about fucking her on the floor of her uncle's bathroom when we were staying over before a wedding. I thought about the way she often liked me to tell her what to do in bed. I thought about the day it first occurred to me that, should she die, there would be no one in the world I truly loved. You can, I think, love someone a very long time before you realize this, notice it in the way you note a facial flaw, a speech impediment, some imperfection which, once recognized, can never again be unseen. *Are you just now realizing that people die*, Leah had said to me when I voiced this thought, tucked up beside her on the sofa with my knees pressed tight into the backs of hers. *Not people*, I had said, *just you*.

At the start of the fourth month of Leah's absence, I witnessed a fracas on the message board for wives of imaginary spacemen. One woman accused another of failing to treat her fantasy with due courtesy and the thread quickly descended into a frenzy of recrimination about how one wife's imaginary trauma stacked up against another's.

MHIS HAS BEEN GONE FOR SEVEN YEARS, one woman posted, *MTP* [Mission to Pluto]. *NO SIGN. NO CONTACT. NOTHING. CREW PRESUMED DEAD. NO HOPE OF RESCUE. THINK ABOUT THAT BEFORE YOU TELL ME MY STORY IS "CONTRIVED."*

I just think, another woman posted in response, *that if you were really so cut up about your husband's absence you wouldn't be posting details here the way you do.*

Check the community guidelines, a third woman, apparently fancying herself site cop, added to the discourse. *Don't come for other people's stories. Offer the same respect you would expect.* "Have Grace in Space."

She says there's been no contact but she posted just last week about her husband sending her one last message while orbiting Pluto, a fourth inserted herself at this point. *We're not saying it's a bad story, we're saying just try to be consistent.*

I read this thread in its entirety over the course of about an hour. Once I'd finished, I drank several glasses of wine in quick succession and typed in the comment box that Pluto was no longer a planet. *fURTHERMORE,* I added, unaware I had clicked on all caps, *IF YOU PEOPLE DON'T WANT YOUR HUSBANDS THEN WHY DO YOU GO TO THE TROUBLE OF MAKING THEM UP IN THE FIRST PLACE.*

Directly after posting this, I closed my laptop and dialed the number I had for the Centre. The call went straight to voice-mail, so I left a message I now remember very little about.

———

I dreamed a lot during that time and in uneasy colors—pale water leaking from the cupboard, the notches from an unfamiliar spine strewn cold across the windowsill. One night, I dreamed a congregation: fifty women in formal hats declaring themselves the acolytes of the *Church of the Blessed Sacrament of Our Wives Under the Sea.* The church was tall, a plunging upward streak of ceiling that leered into the distant vaulted rafters, then fell beneath our feet to corresponding depths. I sat with legs curled up inside a pew and peered into the vast abyss that should have been the floor, the chancel, aisle, and transepts. The space beneath us seethed with almost-movement—dark surge of something otherworldly. The woman who had once asked me about Flat Stanley stood up toward the altar, arms out, her hair flowing oddly upward. The convocation raised their hands in imitation and I looked toward the front, expecting a song, a benediction, a prayer for those long lost. *The USS* Johnston, said the woman at the altar, *is the deepest shipwreck thus far located, at over twenty thousand feet. The known wreckage pieces consist of two turrets, a propeller shaft and propeller, two funnels, a mast, and several unidentified pieces of debris. At the point of sinking, only 141 of the vessel's 327-strong crew were saved. At least 90 managed to disembark the vessel before she sank, but were never seen again.* There was a murmur in the congregation, a sound that I was slow to recognize as *Amen.*

————

In the fifth month, I began to assume she was dead, which made things both easier and harder. I felt nothing and then utterly kneecapped by it, wanted so desperately to know what her last thought had been and whether it had been about me. I called Sam crying but when pressed at first could only say that the cat I'd been looking after had died. *Oh sweetheart,* she said—the warm midnight weight of her voice, distant rustle of duvet covers—*you know my mother used to tell me that cats know when it's time to go. We had one when I was little and one day when she was about sixteen we couldn't find her anywhere, assumed she'd run off. Anyway two days later we found her, all curled up in a box of picnic rugs in the shed at the bottom of the garden. She just knew it was time to take herself off, you know?*

In response to this, I kept on crying and told her I'd made it up, that I didn't know why I'd said that thing about the cat.

I know that, sweetheart, she said to me, *I had a feeling.* Her voice was thick but she kept talking and I think I loved her for that.

LEAH

I'll tell you something: for someone who likes the water, I've never been particularly keen on the dark.

We sat together and stared at the torches, at the thin central reeds of the filaments, which left white lines across the backs of my eyes.

"We submerged at noon," Jelka said at one point, gesturing to her wrist, "but my watch is broken. It's stopped on two forty-five."

It was tricky to tell much in this regard by any normal method; none of us were very hungry or very thirsty or showing much of an impulse to sleep. I had no watch and neither did Matteo, and without power, all the dials and meters and timepieces ranged around the main console were less than useless.

"Could have been days," Matteo said and then shook his head in the manner of someone trying to get water out of their ears, "but that's not really a helpful thing to say, is it?"

"Is it strange," I asked, "that we haven't seen anything yet?" They looked at me and I gestured my head toward the window without moving my eyes from the lights. "However long we've been here, I mean, and we haven't seen a thing."

Matteo laughed, the sound metallic against the ceiling of the craft.

"Well, I don't know what you expect to see, buddy, just staring at that torch for hours."

I nodded, shrugged.

"That's fair enough, I guess, but you haven't seen anything either."

Deep-sea fish are not fish in a way that the average person would recognize. Having evolved to deal with the dark and the pressure, they sprout feelers from unfamiliar places, grow great gulping jaws that overspill the circumference of their bodies, produce their own creeping chemical light. Instead of relying on gas for buoyancy, many deep-sea species simply roll through the water like jelly, unencumbered by an inner or outer skeleton, their bodies made up of compounds of such low density that the pressure of surrounding water poses no threat at all. Some of my favorite deep-sea fish are also some of the strangest-looking: the frilled shark, generally considered a living fossil, with its thirty-odd rows of needlelike teeth; the faceless cusk, which appears to have almost no features at all beyond two pairs of nostrils and a large and bulbous snout. Many deep-sea creatures also have a tendency to gigantism, though this is not a topic on which, so far, there has been a great deal of study. Suffice it to say, there has been a noted tendency in crustaceans and cephalopods retrieved from the deep ocean to be of far greater than usual size, though suggested explanations for this range from lower temperatures to food scarcity and are not generally agreed upon.

All of which is a long-winded way of saying that the deep sea might be dark, but that doesn't make it uninhabited. It certainly *was* strange that however long it had been since we stopped sinking, we had not seen a single thing beyond the glass.

MIRI

"*Let's be serious,*" the therapist says, "*I don't think that either of you are listening hard enough.*"

When she says this, she is talking about me.

"All right," I say, "I'm listening," but this apparently demonstrates my tendency toward belligerence and we have to start the exercise again.

The therapy is free, bankrolled by the Centre on the understanding that further assistance will be forthcoming, although they are somewhat hazy on the details. This was the main thing I managed to sort, on finally getting through to someone on the phone. I tried to mention other things, tried to talk about the obvious changes in Leah, tried to ask for an explanation, but the voice on the line was implacable in the face of my questioning, assuring me several times that prolonged dives could throw up all kinds of issues and that I shouldn't be too concerned. *We call it the resurfacing glitch,* the voice said, so cheerfully that I felt almost churlish for asking. *It's so common, more common than you'd think.*

To begin, the therapist shows us a series of inkblot cards and asks us to say what we see in each butterflying shape.

"A genie," I say, "an ice-cream scoop. Was the Rorschach test not widely discredited around the mid-60s? An enchilada."

"What I see," Leah says, looking hard at each shape, "is an eye, and an eye and an eye and an eye and an eye."

The therapist lays her cards facedown on the coffee table and makes a series of notes in a ring-bound pad before asking me how I feel about my mother. When I say that I'm not quite sure how that could be relevant, she explains that she takes a "deep listening" approach to couples' therapy, adding that childhood experience could often be a root of dysfunction in adult relationships.

"What we'll do here together," she says, "is connect the dots."

I am, apparently, too given to the process of blame. I have allowed blame to settle over me like a weather system, swelling damp inside the curve of my forehead and setting my teeth electric. The therapist tells us to ask each other questions, insists that the silence between us can be broken by something as simple as one of us opening our mouths. I write my questions on index cards as though I am revising for a test and then fold them away somewhere where Leah won't see. *Why*, I write, *did you go if they'd told you to expect all this. What*, I write, *was so fascinating down there that you didn't come back.*

There is something, the therapist says, to be said for letting go of anger. There is something, I tell her in a voice she immediately terms unproductive, to be said for not staying away six months when your operation terms stipulate only three weeks.

It was difficult, in the morning before therapy, to persuade Leah out of the house. She no longer enjoys the process of dressing, finds fabric painful next to her skin, and groans at the prospect of shoes, of walking. On coming home again, I find that a toenail has come clean off inside her walking boots, although she seems unaware of this and moves to sit on the sofa. Without quite knowing what I'm doing, I move over to the sink and spoon a small measure of table salt into a glass of water for Leah to drink.

―――――――

I'm uncertain of the time and therefore uncertain of whether or not it's entirely appropriate for Sam to be here. She's been knocking for several minutes, apparently, and the neighbors had to let her into the building, though there is no sign of them now and their television just switched from a soap opera to the news.

"I just wanted to see if there was anything I could do."

She's brought food, for some reason, wrapped a chicken in tinfoil, producing it from the depths of her bag with an awkward expression. "This looked less strange in my head," she says. "I just thought it might be nice."

It's a bad day, Leah dragging herself about the flat like a grappling hook, catching on the furniture. I take the chicken and ask whether there's any chance of a rain check.

"She's a bit under the weather," I say, like some smiling kidnapper in a horror movie, chatting benignly to the mailman. "I don't want to make anything worse."

"I read about this thing," Sam says, "decompression sickness. I say I read about it, I mean I googled it, which I guess is reading. It affects scuba divers, pilots, astronauts—anyone who works in compressed air. Apparently, nitrogen bubbles form in the blood and the tissues and things when the pressure decreases. When they come up, I mean, from underwater. It causes dizziness, apparently—rashes, fatigue, amnesia, even personality changes. Mad stuff. I don't know why I'm telling you this really. I just thought—you've been saying she's not been well, she's been having trouble adjusting, and I just wondered whether it was something that someone could help with? I mean, not that you wouldn't have thought of that—if it was that. Obviously. I'm not trying to diagnose. It's just you haven't told me much and I thought it would be nice to check. Or not nice but, you know, helpful."

The chicken is hot through the tinfoil and I consider dropping it, consider telling her to fuck off, consider telling her to come in and deal with whatever it is I am failing to deal with.

"I'm sorry," she says, when I don't say anything. "I really am the biggest dick on the planet."

We both look at the chicken between us, juice trickling out of a gap in the tinfoil onto the floor.

Much later, after she's left and I've gone back to doing nothing very much from the region of the sofa, she texts me.

I'm sorry, she says, *I shouldn't have brought you a fucking chicken. I should have brought you a coffee and asked if you wanted to talk.*

———

"I don't think this is OK," I say, on my own, in the bathroom, to nobody. I am scouring around the edge of the bath with a sponge and the scrim that comes away with each stroke is pinkish, less granular than it has been in previous weeks, as though something about it is growing thicker. I try not to get it on my fingers. I'm uncertain of whether or not this matter has any correlation to Leah, to the size or to the shape of her, like a layer removed. She has taken to wearing a large floor-length toweling dressing gown around the flat and it's difficult to get a clear idea of how she looks underneath it, whether this is a shedding or a breaking down.

Look at this, I want to say, imagine holding the sponge to her face and asking for an explanation. I imagine asking her to tell me what the problem is, I imagine asking for a hug. *My Leah wouldn't be like this*, I want to tell her. *She wouldn't be so silent, she wouldn't leave an inch of herself behind whenever she took a bath.*

It is still comforting, of a fashion, to think about my Leah, though such thoughts come attendant on the usual wave of grief that my Leah is not who I have with me now. My Leah was funny and strange and predominantly wore men's underwear. My Leah chewed hangnails loudly and knew the name of every actor yet never remembered the words to a song. My Leah took me out to the beach near the nuclear power station where she'd used to go walking with her father—haar fog in January, too cold and too early for anyone to be there but us. I took my shoes and socks off and cut my feet to pieces on oyster shells trying to seem willing as I ran down to the water. It was that morning that we saw the sea lung, a squint of ice in my throat like a splinter, like something come loose from the air and lodged in my flesh.

I have always thought the edge of the water is somehow particularly cold—a strange almost-place that seems perceptibly to dip in temperature. It is something Leah has always put down to the shifting of the air between two elements, the chilly liminality of water and earth. Standing at the place where one fades into the other, I have always been sure that I feel it: the sudden confusion. The air drawing taut between one stage and another. Looking out across the water and feeling my feet connected to something more solid than the plunging uncertainty beyond, I have always felt weighted, literal, a tangible creature connected to the earth.

The only time I felt something very different to this was when we saw the sea lung. It was a term Leah taught me, that day in fact, grasped my hand and kissed it and told me that "sea lung" was an ancient term once used by sailors to describe the slough of ice that forms on the surface of the ocean when the air changes temperature rapidly enough to freeze water thrown to the surface in choppy weather. The effect created is that of a sort of floating platform—a spread of barely solid water like a vast and drifting jellyfish that sailors once took to be some organ of the sea's internal structure come loose and straining skyward.

I still remember it: a drifting anomaly of matter, solid and yet not quite so, spread out beyond the doom bar. I remember the sensation of my feet on solid ground and my hand in Leah's solid grasp and the disconcerting sight of something almost solid farther out. It seemed, from a distance, to be something one could conceivably walk on, though of course in reality if you set foot on it, it would immediately give way to the water beneath. I turned to Leah and felt an odd sort of relief, despite her hand around mine, to find her still with me, to find she had not moved farther up the beach to search for cowrie shells and left me teetering in this uncertain place. The sea lung moved very slightly, leading me to feel that the ground I stood on might be moving, too, might be less substantial than I assumed. I pressed my free hand to my chest and wondered how solid that could really be, how tangible anything about me might really be. Standing on the edge, I could feel it. The chill of the air, aching to become something else.

LEAH

At some point, Jelka had produced a small plastic figurine of Saint Brendan of Clonfert and set it down beside one of the torches. She now sat on the floor in front of it the way one might huddle around a fireplace, her neck bent to such a degree that the bulging white marbles of her vertebrae showed up like something seeking exit through her skin. She had told me once that you prayed *with* saints, not to them, correcting a turn of phrase I think I must have inherited from Miri, who was a Catholic hobbyist at best. *Praying to a saint would be a gesture of idolatry,* Jelka had said, seeming to smirk at herself but carrying on regardless. *You pray so that a saint will make an intercession to God on your behalf. Spiritually speaking, it's like diving with a buddy.*

Jelka's Catholicism had always been a curious part of her, a white-hot core to a person I otherwise knew to be brisk and rational and often cold-blooded, little given to panic but simultaneously hard to placate once panic had set in. We had worked together frequently on research projects at our old facility, had transferred to the Centre together, and I had always known her to be smarter than me, a little aloof but given to sharing lunches, rarely open about things that Matteo and I discussed freely and often. I was unsure, for instance, if she had any siblings, a partner, parents she cared for: all things about which I typically liked to ask because I knew that Miri would be interested to know. I didn't know if she'd ever been in love, if she considered the concept of love important. I didn't know what it was she might think about Miri and me, as two women together. One thing I did know about Jelka was her saints. As a child, she had been an altar server at her church in central Haarlem and growing up had been blazingly convinced that by the time she hit adulthood, Catholic policy would have bent to oncoming modernity enough to allow her to train as a priest. This having proved incorrect, she had taken the somewhat sideways step of training in marine ecology and conservation and had ultimately spent several years completing fieldwork on the New Caledonian barrier reef before we met. When I asked her once (with a glibness that really should have been embarrassing) if the appeal of the ocean lay, to her, in some sense of religious universality, of God being everywhere, she had shaken her head and told me, *No—what it is is that I'm fucking furious I can't do the thing that I wanted to do, and I feel better in places where there aren't any churches.* I was pretty chastened by this and didn't ask her any personal questions for a long time afterward, which I think is what she'd hoped.

Saint Brendan of Clonfert is the patron saint of mariners; more specifically the patron saint of sailors, divers, adventurers, travelers and, for whatever reason, whales. He was one of several saints I associated particularly with Jelka—one of several saints whose existence I had come to recognize because of her. As a teenager, so she told me once, she had passed through fleeting passions for saints the way most people ran through movie stars, fixating short bursts of ardor upon Saint Erasmus, Saint Augustine, Saint Clare of Assisi, Saint Benedict, Saint Genevieve, and Saint Anne. At the age of thirteen, she had conceived a particular passion for Saint Lidwina, a Dutch mystic partially paralyzed after breaking her rib in a fall on the ice. This fall, so a teenaged Jelka had read with the breathlessness that accompanies a crush, precipitated a lifetime of physical hardship, from gangrene and bleeding from the nose and mouth, to parts of the body falling off, to blindness and even stigmata. *My favorite part of the story*, she told me, *was that she fasted. She was in that much pain, bits of her skin coming away, pieces of her body, and she was still so devout that she fasted for God. I was a bloodthirsty little bitch when you think about it. I loved that so much. I read this book once that said that all she ate were apples and dates and all she drank was salt water.*

I remember the way she told this story, the way she touched a hand to her lips directly afterward, as though checking for excess moisture.

Saint Brendan is less of a horror story, although no less compelling in its way. An Irish saint and seafarer, he sailed the Atlantic in search of the Garden of Eden, encountering devils, gryphons, and sea monsters. Jelka told me this story while half-asleep, a long time ago. Midnight on the coral triangle, the two of us bunking together on a trip. We were working for a conservationist project in tandem with our old facility, collecting data on biofluorescence in cryptic fish species, and the hours were long, leading to curious, overtired conversations that simultaneously rambled and went nowhere. *There are different stories*, I remember she said, tight voiced, moving her hands through the darkness, *sometimes the journey is his own quest for the holy land and sometimes the journey's a punishment. He does something wrong and so an angel sets him out onto the ocean and makes him sail for nine years. Heavy-handed, but then things to do with angels usually are.*

In the sea, in the dark, there isn't time—not in the way you would ordinarily perceive it. It can be hard to force your body into working order, hard to recognize the natural breaks between awake and asleep, aware and unconscious. Of course, there are typically ways to combat this, protocols that submariners follow: maintaining a twenty-four-hour watch schedule, operating a light system that cycles through various stages of brightness and dimness, dependent on time of day. Without this kind of assurance, the circadian rhythms can swiftly begin to break down. A few days can be all it takes. As we were now, without power in our sunken craft, it would become very hard, very quickly, to keep things from going awry.

I sat with Jelka and looked at the silhouette of the saint where it sat against the torchlight. At some point I must have slept, though I'm unclear as to exactly when this started.

MIRI

I didn't date as a teenager, missed the boat due in part to an excess of panic. At the age of thirteen I became obsessed with venereal diseases, misunderstood my way into a locked box from which I then spent the rest of my teens attempting to extract myself. At some point, I had come to understand that somewhere at the core of sex as an activity lay the possibility not only of illness but specifically of bodily harm, and this con-viction, once formed, proved difficult to shake.

My school years consisted predominantly of sweating through my shirts and obsessing over physical contact. I spent hours mentally constructing the pressure of a hand on my knee, pressed the crease of my thumb and forefinger into the side of my neck to simulate kissing, comprehensively failed to learn how to masturbate. I thought confusedly and often of a girl who sat in front of me in Geography, imagined us becoming close friends, so close that everyone else in our year was jealous. I neglected to deal with the hair on my upper lip while ritualistically waxing my underarms upward of six times a month. I thought a lot about the men from the movies I en-joyed but mostly in the context of their being eaten by sharks or falling from high buildings or otherwise breaking apart. At the age of eighteen, for reasons unknown to me now, I allowed a boy named Jeremy Fox to kiss me at an end-of-term party and afterward spent several weeks imagining him biting my arm until the blood came, which of course he hadn't done. At the age of twenty-two, I kissed a boy at a university bar whose name I forget but whose methods I still remember: strong yank to the back of my neck and all his teeth at once, as though he were using me to floss with. The men I kissed were typically of middle height, dark haired, and gently anodyne. I worked my way up to the giving of occasional hand jobs and even more occasional blow jobs and panicked for weeks afterward about what I might have caught. I refused to have penetrative sex with any of them, imagined sex as a kind of battering, and after a while they went away with little in the way of hard feelings. At the age of twenty-four, I went on an internet date with a man who kissed me hard against the railing of a bridge and told me conversationally that he was a dom, but then grew upset when I told him to stop pulling my hair. *I don't feel safe with you*, he said and didn't call me again. When I told this story to Leah, years later, she told me he couldn't have been the right kind of dom. *They can be difficult to find*, she said, took the inside of my wrist and kissed it, then smiled when I told her I thought I'd said to keep her arms above her head. *Maybe he was just sensing that the two of you weren't compatible.*

Sex with Leah was a key and a lock, an opening up of something I had assumed impassable, like a door warped shut by the heat. Joy in the fact of pleasure, in the fact of my own relief. When we fucked, I felt myself distinct from my previous versions: the frenzied me, the panicked me, the me who had imagined herself poisoned by something she had never even done. *I don't think*, Leah said to me once, *that the problem was really you.* She was lying beneath me—her light hair, her strong chin, the way she had of widening her eyes when I came too close, as if to encompass the whole of me better—and when I made a questioning noise she kissed the side of my face. *I just mean*, she said, *that being afraid of sex isn't typically anyone's fault, it's just a question of circumstance.*

The last time before she went away (the last time full stop), I pushed her into the mattress and held her there, pressed my palm into the indent of her throat and then released, and then pressed again. (*Hold my throat when I come*, she had said to me once, *that way you can feel the noises before I make them.*) It was light still—forgetful afternoon, charmed hour before the coming on of evening. The going-away party was scheduled for the next night. *Shall we pretend I'm going to war*, she said, and I laughed and bit the insides of her thighs the way she liked me to and later on she kissed me and crooked her fingers inside me, twisted them around almost 180 degrees, the way we had discovered, through trial and error, was the only way that worked. I remember her legs, the smudge of green bruises, synthetic citrus smell of her underarms. I remember the way that her hair rose static from the crown and then fell again. I remember the way that she looked at me, the open surge of her gaze, like I was something she'd invented, brought to life by the powers of electricity and set down there, in the last of the light.

Carmen is eating toast, tells me I should see somebody about that look on my face.

"Chronic bitch face is naturally distinct from resting bitch face, you know. It's like a whole different ball game when you can't turn it off."

She's had some good news about her eyesight, might be eligible for experimental surgery that will aim to reverse the degeneration. She squints at a triangle of toast through her glasses, spreads her free hand beside it. "My hand looks like toast. Everything looks like toast," she says and pushes away from the table to order another coffee at the counter.

When she gets back, she is bearing a coffee for me as well as one for herself. She sets it down in front of me as a sort of peace offering.

"I'm sorry I said that about your face," she says, quite earnestly, gesturing to her own eyes. "What do I know anyway?"

It occurs to me that I ought to apologize to her, though for what I'm not quite sure. I feel angry at nothing, ashamed at myself for using her as one of my few escapes from the flat. I look down at the coffee she's brought me, its chocolate-dusted heart already sinking into the foam. I think about Sam and wonder why everyone seems so set on bringing me coffee.

Later on, back home, I become briefly convinced that Leah has vanished. I move from room to room, checking wardrobes, opening drawers, and upsetting piles of clothes from the armchairs on which I've allowed them to gather. I check the latch of the bathroom window, stare for several unhinged seconds at the drain in the base of the sink, but then there she is, of course, standing in the bathroom doorway in her floor-length dressing gown as though nothing has happened, and I can't understand how I missed her.

"I wonder, Miri," says the therapist, *"whether you have* properly taken the time to imagine what it is your wife has been through. There is a difference, of course, between understanding and forgiving and I don't believe one necessarily prompts the other, but it might be easier for you to cope with

the fact of *now* if you choose to contend with the truth of before."

The therapist is tall and straight, both in the sense of her sexuality and in the sense of her everything else. When she makes notes during the session, her handwriting rises and falls without listing; her talk is long and thin; she stirs her coffee with the flat of a knife.

"I don't understand," I reply, looking at the side of Leah's face with an attempt at frankness that I hope is mirrored in my tone, "because she never tells me anything. I know you went away and I know you stayed longer than you meant to and I know you must miss it now, or else why do you run the taps all night and carry your sound box everywhere you go? Problem is I don't know what it is you miss, I don't know what it is at all."

"What is it you imagine," Leah says to me, though her eyes are now on the therapist, "what is it you imagine when you think about where I was?"

I look at her for a long moment before pushing myself up out of my chair and crossing to the bookshelf by the door. I take the thickest book I can find from the shelf and carry it back to the coffee table, pull a slip of paper from my own handbag, and hold it up for a moment before sliding it between the very last page of the book and the back cover. Then I allow the whole heavy weight of the three hundred or so preceding pages plus front cover to fall shut. The slip of paper sticks out between the final page and back cover like a bookmark and I think of how I felt on the viewing deck years ago, when she left not for this last trip but for another, the thing I wished I'd said louder: *I'm not sure a ship like that can take the whole of the ocean on top of it, I'm not sure they can all go down that deep and not be crushed.*

"This is how I imagine it," I say and watch as Leah's eyes travel slowly from the therapist to rest upon the book with the little strip of paper crushed beneath the weight of its pages.

We have to catch the bus back from the therapist's office, and on the journey back, Leah nearly loses her footing climbing up to the top deck, claiming afterward that she suddenly lost sensation in her hands.

"Just the fingertips," she says when I press her, allowing me to take hold of her hands and examine them, though after a moment the feeling appears to become too much for her and she pulls them away. She is dressed in loose trousers, a long-sleeved shirt with a high collar. Beneath her shirt, the bones of her shoulders swing the way a hanger will when knocked inside a wardrobe. When she talks, her tongue is white, indented with tooth marks, though in truth these days she talks less and less.

When Leah was gone, when I became convinced that she had died and no one had thought to tell me, I grew briefly obsessed with a website for people whose loved ones had disappeared. It was better and worse than the message board for the wives of imaginary spacemen, inasmuch as the conversation was typically less ridiculous but the stories universally worse. The people who posted were mourning the losses of lovers and siblings, parents in the throes of dementia who had wandered away from secure facilities, sisters who had run off in stolen hatchbacks, friends who had simply vanished, the way that people often do. I say *mourning*, though of course the abstract of grief is different without a body, without a point from which to hang the solid object of one's pain. *Does anyone else find the possibility of the comeback kind of worse than the idea of death*, someone posted. *Not that you don't want them to return but rather that that's the tormenting thing: the thought that they might do.*

Something I learned very quickly was that grieving was complicated by lack of certainty, that the hope inherent in a missing loved one was also a species of curse. People posted about children who had gone missing upward of fifteen years ago and whose faces were now impossible to conjure, about friends who had messaged to confirm a meeting place and then simply never showed up. In almost every case, the sense of loss was convoluted by an ache of possibility, by the almost-but-not-quite-negligible hope of reprieve. Deus ex machina—the missing loved one thrown back down to earth. Grief is selfish: we cry for ourselves without the person we have lost far more than we cry for the person—but more than that, we cry because it helps. The grief process is also the coping process and if the grief is frozen by ambiguity, by the constant possibility of reversal, then so is the ability to cope.

It's not grief, one woman posted, *it's more like a haunting.* Her sister had disappeared two decades previously, run away or otherwise removed via the back door of their childhood home when she was fifteen years old. *There was no proof that anything bad had happened*, the woman typed, *no proof of anything at all. They told us hope wasn't lost so often that it became impossible to live with it. It's too hard, trying to exist between these poles of hope and death. You just find yourself imagining all these possibilities, all these possible sisters wandering around half-unseen like people with sheets over their head, except that somewhere among them, you know that one of them's real—one of them's dead, one of them's the ghost.*

I found I liked this woman, read her updates with particular interest and scrolled the website in the early morning, as this appeared to be her favorite time to post. More than once, I found myself building up to writing her a message, typing sentences that I then deleted, refashioned, deleted again.

I used to hope, I typed once, *that I'd die before my partner, even though I knew that was selfish. I used to think that I hoped I'd die before she died and before the planet died and really just generally before things got any worse.*

I didn't send this message, specifically because it seemed to imply that my views had changed, when they hadn't.

LEAH

I had slept, and when I had, I had dreamed about Miri. I saw the warm dark, the changing light of the aquarium at which I had worked in my teens. In the dream, Miri held my hand by the Open Ocean tank, pulled me down onto a viewing bench, and kissed me just beneath my collar. *I love it here,* she said, *I love the way it moves.* I opened my mouth to tell her about all the different species she could find in the tank and she shook her head, clapped her hand to my lips. *Don't do that,* she said, though my mouth was already leaking water. I had woken shortly after that. I didn't want to sleep again until I had to.

Time passed. I don't know how much or how quickly. We changed the batteries in the torches and ate because there was food in the lockers and we knew we ought to eat it. At some point, Jelka lay down on the floor of the main deck and went to sleep. Matteo sat by the comms deck, idly pressing and re-pressing the transmission button, and at one point began to whistle *Farewell and adieu to you fair Spanish ladies* again. I sat on the floor beside Jelka, stretched my legs out, and thought about showering. They had made a big fuss of the wash stall the first time they showed us around the craft, a woman from the Centre throwing open the door to present us with the sink, the toilet, and the showerhead like someone on a home makeover show revealing a lavish en suite bath. *The distillation system is state-of-the-art,* the woman said, rubbing a cuff across the shower dial like you might do with a new car. *Brings the water in from the outside and purifies it. Maximum efficiency, as much fresh water as you need. No Navy showers here—theoretically you could keep the shower on for hours without encountering problems. Turn the tap on in the sink, too, if you like. Have a party!* I had nodded at her, watched her continue to buff at the shower dial for several seconds before moving back into the rear chamber.

Now, on the floor of the main deck, I turned the image of the shower dial over in my mind. If the shower still worked, then we still had fresh water. If we still had fresh water, then things were not quite critical yet. It occurred to me that, given the CO_2 scrubbers were still running, there was every chance the water-distillation function was still operational, too. I decided to note this as a positive, though I delayed the act of actually getting up and checking until it was absolutely necessary. No reason to think the worst until it was actually happening.

Propped up beside my legs, Jelka was frowning in her sleep. I wasn't sure why we hadn't gone through to the rear chamber, which was altogether more comfortable. Perhaps we assumed that the second we did, the comms deck would spring to life, unnoticed, and that whoever was calling for us would assume we were lost and switch off.

Matteo was technically the engineer, though all three of us had been trained to a level that we ought to have been able to fix whatever was wrong. The problem, of course, was that nothing *was* wrong, aside from the fact of the obvious. We were all breathing normally, there was no indication that the craft was failing to bear up to external pressure. As Matteo had already found, there were no obvious faults, no flashing lights, no jams in the system. The craft had slowed itself down prior to impact with the ground, as though following a command it should no longer have been capable of following. Aside from the fact that we were unable to move in any direction and unable to communicate, it was really a ten-out-of-ten maiden voyage.

———————

Have you ever heard of the Tektite habitat? This was an underwater laboratory and living station designed and built round about the late 1960s as a base from which to study marine life. Closely resembling a pair of connected grain silos, it sat at seabed level at Great Lameshur Bay and was used in preparation for NASA's Apollo missions from early 1969, when the moon landing was just months away. In the main, NASA used the base to study the behavior and psychology of small crews living in extreme close quarters and the biomedical responses to long stretches spent in oxygen-controlled conditions, not unlike those of a spacecraft. Several teams were sent down to live for ten- or twenty-day stretches underwater, though my favorite among these has always been the team led by Sylvia Earle—a renowned biologist and explorer—which also happened to be the first all-female saturation dive team in history. I read about this in my father's diving almanac and again in a book I once stole from his study called *A Hundred and One Deep-Sea Dives of Note*. In a team consisting of four scientists and one engineer, Earle's crew spent two weeks underwater, documenting marine plant life while at the same time being studied themselves, both for their behavior in isolation and, in a frankly unavoidable way, for their choice of swimwear. *They called us the aquababes*, Earle said once, in an article I cut out and kept, *the aquanaughties, all sorts of things*. On emerging from the water, they were an immediate media sensation, with the focus squarely on their wet suits and bikinis and really the inescapable Bond girl–sexiness of the whole thing, of these women and their underwater lair.

Among the many things my father collected, he had a stash of old *New Yorker* magazines, dating back as far as 1972. He kept these in a series of old wine crates that he stacked in his garage and periodically allowed me to root through, I assume to get me out of his hair. I was thirteen when I found a copy from July 1989 that contained a profile of Sylvia Earle. Entitled "Her Deepness," it was a detailed rundown of a long and wildly impressive life of deep-sea exploration, and I immediately whisked it away to read. One of my favorite parts of the article, the whole of which I read seven or eight times in the space of one weekend, was when Earle talked about the Tektite habitat, explaining that the Washington review committee in charge of selecting teams to man the station hadn't actually expected women to apply at all. *There were still some remarkably prudish attitudes in Washington in those days*, she said, *and the people in charge just couldn't cope with the idea of men and women* living together *underwater*. It was seemingly for this reason, really more than any desire to push the envelope, that the first female dive team was born. *It makes sense when you think about it*, my father said when I brought the article to him, *actually a pretty neat solution to a problem. Really they should take this into account with space exploration, too. No chance of crewmates getting involved with each other when it's all women—no distraction, no nookie, no silly buggers. Clever in its way.*

I said nothing to this, although later on I lay and thought about these women, imagined myself a crewmate aboard the Tektite—the ghostly shoals of fish beyond the bubbled portholes, the tangled kelp, the stillness, the sudden scuds of light.

Now, on the floor of the main deck, I thought about this

again, tried to remember the longest any team had submerged on the Tektite, the longest it was advisable to submerge.

"Do you smell it?" Jelka said, and I looked down at her, unsure of how long she had been awake.

"Smell what?" Matteo said, though his expression did not match the question, as though he already knew the answer. It was the smell of something burning, of meat straight off the bone.

MIRI

I run beside the canal in the early mornings and afterward I usually go to the café near the municipal leisure center, where I drink two coffees in quick succession before heading back. There is a man at the café by the leisure center who has on at least three occasions written his number down on my receipt when I've paid for my coffees. I'm not entirely sure why he keeps doing this when at no point has it yielded results—perhaps he believes that as yet I simply haven't noticed, perhaps he's just a sexual predator—but either way, he does it again this morning as I hand over my change. I am briefly annoyed at the whole situation, briefly alarmed, and then it occurs to me that all I need to do is tell him I have a girlfriend (which is not true, I have a wife, but people seem to find that cute in a way they don't when I just say *girlfriend*). I look at him for several seconds, holding my coffees in both hands and not saying anything, and then I say to him, abruptly, "Please stop doing that," and leave without taking my receipt.

This happened once, a long time ago: Leah and I on an early date and a man in between us at the bar, forcing a leg between our stools with the forward-thrusting motion of someone preventing an elevator door from closing. *Are you sisters*, he had said, and she told him *yes* and then kissed my open mouth.

————

Leah is in the bathroom, the sound machine playing, the phone ringing. My bad tooth is aching, though I'm doing my best to ignore it. Our quarterly water bill is in the region of twelve times above average and I have no clear idea of how we're going to pay it.

I've been going through the papers from Leah's transfer to the Centre, trying to make sense of a number of things I thought I already knew. I am unsure, for instance, of exactly when it was that Leah's job became obscure to me, when I stopped knowing what it was she was doing on a daily basis while still assuming I did. I am thinking, again, about the going-away party, about the people there I didn't know. I am thinking about a man Leah described in joking terms as "The Boss," as though she were referring to Bruce Springsteen, pointing out a man in pressed jeans and a sports jacket who didn't make a speech when others did, but afterward ate a total of twelve cocktail sausages from the buffet table and apologized when he jostled me en route to the salad bowl. I remember him the way I think you often remember unimportant things: too clearly and in too much detail. The way your memory will relinquish important things yet conjure the bright sense of a boring landscape or a throwaway conversation, so I remember the dark upward sweep of his hair and the etched insignia on his ring, like the lines of an eye. I remember the way he stepped back politely to give me space and asked if I'd enjoyed the party, and I remember, too, the way that shortly afterward he departed without ceremony and no one commented on the fact that he had gone. *We are prouder than ever before*, a woman from the Centre declared into a microphone, *of all we as a company have achieved, and more certain than ever before that we stand*

at the vanguard of further discovery. We know already that life exists
everywhere, even in the places as yet inaccessible, and we know, too,
that that life has things to teach us and must be sought out.

---

*I see my mother in myself, though less in the sense of inher-*ited features and more in the sense of an intruder poorly hid-den behind a curtain. I see her impatience in the skin of my neck, her anger in the way my hands move. I see her when I press my tongue into the inside of my cheek with irritation yet refuse to do anything to make a situation better. I see her when I assume people are worse than they turn out to be.

When my mother used to smile, a rarity, the skin at the sides of her mouth rippled back like a stone thrown into water. In physical terms, there is nothing to a smile: twelve to thirteen muscles, give or take. Teeth only optional. I read somewhere, probably online, that a Duchenne smile denotes contraction of the zygomatic major muscle in conjunction with the or-bicularis oculi, otherwise known as *smiling with the eyes*. A smile is voluntary and typically brief, lightning split across the face. It costs you almost nothing, but my mother nonetheless trained herself almost entirely out of it, believing it puckered the skin and loosened the facial muscles. Frowning, too, and raising the eyebrows were both things that she avoided, citing magazines that advised against yawning too widely, ironing her index fingers over the places where undue emotion had caused the skin of her forehead to crease. What remained was an impassivity—white lines about the underside of her lip that she smoothed away with cold cream. She spoke from the cen-ter of her mouth, patched the creases that formed around her eyes with concealer the color of crafting glue. When she swal-

lowed, her throat moved as if in protest at her face's immobil-
ity, swelling and contracting with such force that her head was
not infrequently thrown back.

When she became ill, much of this self-imposed rigidity
was lost, my mother's face untethered but suddenly uncon-
trolled. She became prone to involuntary facial and bodily
spasms, struggled to regulate her body's speed, its movement
through space, its sudden dislocating stops. It became crueler,
unwatchable. She ceased to obey herself, her jaw hanging
loose and then tightening, skin buckling up in ways she could
no longer prevent. I saw it and felt sick. When I went to visit
her, I found it increasingly difficult not to imagine the two of
us breaking down and turning to dust, just at slightly different paces. Her first and then me. *Don't you dare*, she said to
me once, though her speech was caught up in the back of her
throat as if somehow half-digested, *don't you dare look at me that
way*. I didn't know how I was looking, so I looked at the floor
and shortly after that I went home.

Things I remember: my mother, eating honey on toast,
commenting on the number of fat people she had seen at the
supermarket; her juicing machine, its blades fanned upward;
the way she wrote my name on the insides of my school shoes;
the tight white trick of her hair, at once blond and gray and
silver; the first frightened slip of her memory, before we knew
what was wrong, and she called her neighbor's cat Cassandra,
though the neighbor's cat had no name and Cassandra was the
name my mother had once thought of giving me; her wrists,
her hands, and the way she drew them into her sleeves as
though insulted; her Tae Bo videos; the strange sleepwalking
manner in which she occasionally stood at the kitchen counter
and stirred her index finger around the peanut-butter jar; the

sound of her opening up a crab at the breakfast table, the gills
and digestive organs strewn between the plates; the fact that
she was always thinner than me and worked at it; her feet; the
gentle grasp and then drop of a hug that I'd initiated; the sun
hat she kept on the phrenology head in the hall; her blue eyes
and smell like eiderdown; the fact she died during the two-
minute silence in November, the lack of care she gave to the
plans of others extending even to the Armistice; her contradictory stance on almost everything; the time when I was seven
and she leaned out of the window of her car to shout at a boy
who'd called me a bitch on the playground; the fact of her
face behind my face; the way she asked about Leah only twice
and then stopped asking; her fingernails embedded in me, far
past the point of safe removal.

The phone rings too late to be good news, though when I
pick it up the news is nothing and no one is speaking at all.
This has happened a couple of times in recent weeks and each
time the call is from a private number. In the morning, I call
Carmen and ask whether she was trying to get in touch with
me the night before.

"Not me," she says. "And anyway, you have my number—if
it was me calling, you'd know."

"Well, were you maybe calling from a private number and
you just didn't notice?"

"No, definitely not."

"But are you absolutely sure?"

"I didn't call you last night, Miri, I was watching the pottery
show. Then I went to bed."

Carmen is obsessed with a television show where a group

of contestants construct clay and pottery likenesses of different celebrity guests and are judged in terms of accuracy, artistic merit, and level of offense caused to the celebrity in question. I've never watched it, although I have occasionally heard my neighbors watching it. I couldn't say, on the strength of this, whether it's a show I'd recommend.

"I'm worried about you, Miri," Carmen is saying now, "you're beginning to sound a bit Joan Crawford."

I tell her I'm fine, that last night's call was probably just from an insurance company, or someone jerking off. Carmen asks if I want to come around and watch reruns of the pottery show with her but I tell her I have to look after Leah and hang up.

"Did you know," Leah says, when I turn to look at her, "that seabirds eat more plastic relative to their size than any other animal in the ocean."

She is sitting on the sofa, face tilted toward the windows, and when I ask what she's talking about she doesn't answer. I come over and sit beside her on the sofa, wonder about trying to take her hand. She is swaddled in her floor-length dressing gown, hunkered down, the wishbone span of her shoulders beneath the terry cloth. I find I want to measure her, get up and fetch a length of measuring tape from the kitchen, bring it back and kneel on the sofa at Leah's side.

"Come here," I say, and she looks at me.

When we decided to get married, I took the same tape measure to gauge Leah's ring size and having done so, decided to measure all of her, wrapping the metal strip around her waist and her upper thighs and the place where one bicep was bigger than the other, measuring the line of her clavicles and the distance between each fingertip and the floor. I noted each of these measurements down on a piece of paper and kept it, joking that it would allow me to reconstruct a perfect imitation Leah, should I ever happen to lose her. Of course, I ultimately just ended up losing the paper with the measurements. Somewhere, between throwing out old furniture, between an afternoon's innocuous cleanup, it simply passed out of existence the way things will do and it never even really occurred to me to mind.

I measure Leah again now—the limited parts I can reach outside the dressing gown—wrap the strip around her wrists and upper throat and forehead, take the length of her collarbone and the distance between her nose and cheekbones and chin. I am thinking about the sides of the bath as I do this, about the indeterminate matter that I find myself scrubbing at day after day, about a certain mutability in Leah's stride and looks and presence, a certain ebbing, about the way I don't always hear her when she comes into the room. I note everything down, but having done so I find I can't tell whether these new measurements mean anything—whether Leah is smaller or lesser or different—since I don't remember the measurements I took before.

The therapist agrees to see us over Skype, as Leah has been complaining more often about a lack of sensation in her feet and fingertips and doesn't want to make the trip. I tell the therapist I'm finding it difficult to take things seriously, that I'm finding it difficult to act as though any of what's happening is real.

"You're finding it difficult to connect," she says, and writes something down, and then the internet connection on her end stutters like the punch line to a lazy joke. "I should say," she adds when her picture readjusts, "that I really would find it easier to speak to the pair of you. This kind of therapy can't work when only one of you is present."

I explain to her that Leah is in the bathroom, has been in the bathroom with the door locked since the previous evening, in fact, which is new.

LEAH

I don't know who I'm writing this for, really. I think I need to explain what happened, but it's hard when so much of it happened in the dark. I need to talk about the days, and not knowing what was a day, not knowing how to keep track or what it was that separated night from morning, not knowing how to keep ourselves from going mad.

The noise first started at night—or really what we referred to as night, since it came long enough after an equally arbitrary stretch of daytime. A sudden creak around the southmost side of the craft, a long, wide, billowing motion. It was a noise that seemed to pulse and then retract, like a beating, like the back-and-forth of wings, or of swimming—a noise I can't really explain.

We had moved into the rear chamber by this point and were sitting around the table. Sometime previously, I had checked the shower in the wash stall and found it still in operation, the water running and evidently free of salt. *That's something anyway,* Jelka had said when I reported this, slipping past me into the stall to turn the shower on and tilt her head back, opening her mouth. We had eaten, of a fashion, cleaned up after ourselves. At one point, Matteo had folded down one of the bunks and settled down, as if to sleep, only to get straight up again.

When the noise first came, Matteo suggested whales and Jelka argued that whales would never dive so deep.

"We don't know how deep we are," Matteo said, and Jelka

shrugged at him, pushed a hand through the hair at her temples, still damp from the shower.

"Still doesn't mean it's whales. I've never heard a whale that sounds like that."

The noise seemed to shiver and retreat for a moment, a long wail that faded down into something more like a grinding, like the pull and give of something caught between teeth. I thought about the dark beyond the windows and said nothing, shook my head at the tingle of fright that sat poised at the base of my spine and preparing to struggle higher. The ocean, I had to remind myself, was a place I felt safe, and thinking about the ocean was the method by which I felt safest. When the noise returned, this time on the opposite side of the craft and louring inward (leering inward? swooning inward? It's hard, in retrospect, to assign a tone), I closed my eyes and thought about the shifting shell-soft texture of an octopus mantle, and after a while I felt better, opening my eyes again to find that Matteo and Jelka were still arguing about whether or not the noise might be a whale. I started to say something but at this point there was a rattle around the base of the craft, a hum and screech that seemed to come from somewhere against the exterior structure, beyond the lower hatch leading to the escape trunk, as though something were knocking to be let in.

There have been all sorts of "unexplained sounds" recorded in deep water, and almost all of these are actually just the sounds of glaciers calving, the aftershocks of ice sheets moving over land. Miri used to watch programs that made much of these so-called mysteries, docu-style American deep dives into popular phenomena that always ended on a note of jittery speculation: *So is there a simple explanation, or is it something altogether more sinister? Only you can decide.* Miri would grin at me at the conclusion of these programs, nod her head very seriously, and pretend to be convinced. *You're no fun*, she would say when I explained to her the process of seabed gouging, the sounds emitted when the keel of an iceberg drifts into shallower water and scrapes along the bottom of the sea. *Yeah*—she would nod—*or maybe it's octopus people like the show said.* All of which is to say that sounds, in deep water, are not unexpected, and often far more easily explained than you'd think. We weren't *scared*, is what I'm really trying to say here. We had far more pressing things to be alarmed about and as yet unexplained.

Pushing back her bench, Jelka stood and walked over to the lower hatch, tapped her toe against the handwheel, and frowned. The escape trunk sat at the base of the craft and operated in a manner similar to any air lock, sealed off from the main body of the ship and designed to match the air pressure on the outside, which would allow the outer door to be opened. In our current situation, of course, it was completely useless, as opening the outer door to deep-sea water pressure would result in whoever was in the escape trunk being instantly crushed. This was not an expedition that had ever anticipated any one of us going outside. Our brief had been strictly to observe and map any life we encountered, not to collect or take back. Even so, there could be no theoretical harm in opening up the inner hatch to check what was down there, whether some piece of machinery had come loose or something in one of the drain valves was causing the sound that continued to wail up through the floor. Jelka tapped her toe against the handwheel a second time, tilted back on one heel, and stepped away, still frowning downward.

"Don't be daft," she said, though no one had said anything, and shortly after this she came back to the table and sat down with her back to the hatch.

MIRI

I knock on the bathroom door, then wander through to the bedroom where I stand for a minute, picking things up and putting them down again, drawing my toe in circles through the carpet of hair that has formed over the actual carpet. I haven't been cleaning in here—it feels so specifically Leah's space now—and everything seems unpleasantly furred over and unwashed. I have always been neater than Leah, although in the old days, much of this was simply due to my being at home more consistently. I wore it as a badge of honor, nonetheless, picking up abandoned glasses with a sigh and ferrying them to the dishwasher. *I don't really think it's that hard*, I used to say a lot, and she would apologize and fill the kitchen sink with soap suds, and really, now I think about it, what an absolute waste of life.

I don't realize that Leah has emerged from the bathroom and is standing behind me until I half turn, catch her shadow in the corner of my eye and jump.

"Fucking hell."

She doesn't move, only frowns at me briefly before crossing to the bed and sitting down. I think about being cold in the mornings, about pushing my feet down beneath the bedsheets and finding hers. I think about Leah taking off her makeup in bed, the blurry crescents of mascara across the cotton discs that she would ball on the bedside table.

"Come over here," she says, and I'm surprised but do as I'm told. I sit beside her on the bed and let our shoulders brush, then lean away again, this gentle touch and then removal. I feel for a moment that I understand the whole bright dailiness of our life before this: the morning glances at the bathroom sink, the spit of toothpaste, the cramp and comfort of our hall and living room and kitchen—understand it and also understand that it is gone.

I lean away and she doesn't follow me, clamshelled in her dressing gown and scratching idly at the inside of one arm.

"I was thinking that it's unfair of me," she says, "to hog this bedroom when it isn't only mine."

I say nothing and she nods as though I have.

"I was thinking," she says, "that you can have it if you want. I don't mind switching."

I look at her, think of saying, *I don't think switching would make a difference*, think of saying, *Why don't you just sleep in the bath—you spend enough time there as it is*, say none of this.

"I'm fine," I tell her and she nods and continues to scratch at her arm. I'm surprised when she leans back against me, her toweling shoulder touching mine again, her head dipping into the crook of my neck and holding there. I don't know what to say to this, really. It isn't that we haven't touched since she came back—between one thing and another, I've touched her often, though this has chiefly been in the form of blood mopped up and hair held back as she vomited water. This is different. I find it difficult to remember the feeling of recipro-cation, difficult to locate the muscle memory required of me. I let my head tilt sideways, touch my cheek to the top of her head, find that I badly want to cry.

"I think," she says, "that there's something that's seriously wrong with me. I keep thinking about Jelka. I keep thinking about what we thought we were doing down there."

"What are you talking about?" I say, but she only shakes her head.

She is still scratching at the inside of her arm and this time she shows me, pulls the sleeve of her robe back farther than I have seen in forever, reveals the changing texture of skin, the rubbed-raw glint of something unfamiliar.

"What's that?" I ask, and she shakes her head, pulls up her other sleeve, then parts the floor-length folds of the dressing gown to show me her legs, pulls the cord at the waist, and shows me everything. It is not at all what I expected, all those times when I looked at the scuffed-off particles of matter in the bathtub and imagined her flayed and fraying beneath her clothes. It is something else, and I don't know what to call it or what to say. I look at her and think, briefly, of the strange oyster sheen of her underarms and elbow creases in the first long weeks of her return, of the way she had shown me and said, with a bland sort of certainty, that she'd been told it would go away. I think, too, about the way she had bled, from the face and the gumline, so many mornings of bleeding that have since petered out, as though there might be no more blood to lose.

Now, from midcalf to upper thigh, along her sides and then across her breasts and up along her arms to midforearm, she is at first surf-white, uncertain, and then changing as I look at her, white to blue to green—her skin a drifting texture, somehow unmoored, as though it only floats upon the surface of her flesh.

"I think we need to get you to a doctor," I say, in a useless tone that she seems barely to register.

"I don't feel very good," she says, as though I haven't spoken, and now that I have seen her I know that her voice is not the same, but rather a voice that seems to drown in air, unused to oxygen. "I think," she says, "that there was too much water. When we were down there. I think we let it get in." I look at her and see the way her eyes appear to spill their irises, the way the pulse throbs hard in her throat and at her wrists, as if in answer to some failing inner rhythm.

A bright knife of memory: my mother, holding her hands out flat in front of her. The tremor that wouldn't subside when she willed it, the finger and thumb that wouldn't respond to her efforts to pinch them together. *I feel wrong*, she had said— her voice clear in a way it increasingly seemed not to be—and I'd registered the impulse to throw my arms around her, to struggle against whatever was happening, to tell her I'd make it all right.

"I think," I say to Leah, "I think we should take you back to the bathroom," and I don't know why I say this, really, except that when the bathtub has been filled and I have eased her down into the water, she seems less troubled. She ducks her head, the throbbing at her throat and wrists recedes from view. I kneel beside the bath and watch her shift herself, the pull and shrink of skin around her knees and ankles, the color taking on new shades—first white, then blue, then something else. I look around the bathroom and think about nothing, really. Stupid things. The way I always used to floss and brush and mouthwash where Leah only brushed. The way I used to sit on the edge of the bath and read to her and drink beer while she washed her hair with water poured from a plastic vase, because she preferred it to standing up in the shower. The way she never managed to wash the conditioner out of the tops of her ears.

I look at her now and know what has been true since she

returned: this change, this dragging tide beneath her surface. I watch the water dribble from the corner of her mouth and do not know whether it is simply bathwater or something spilling from inside. I take a flannel and wipe her, gently, cup her head and wonder what it is I feel beneath my palm that isn't hair or skull but something other.

I used to imagine the sea as something that seethed and then quieted, a froth of activity tapering down into the dark and still. I know now that this isn't how it goes, that things beneath the surface are what have to move and change to cause the chain reaction higher up.

Abyssal Zone

LEAH

Matteo slept, and then I did, and when I did I dreamed in an odd, compressed fashion, as though there were too much water on top of me for my thoughts to move about in their usual way. I dreamed about long corridors and about my own spine and about Miri drawing a finger down my neck and then stopping, and when I woke my vision had retracted to a couple of pinholes and everything took several minutes to adjust. We tried the comms panel again and again, we took apart the main deck piece by piece in search of what had gone wrong. We discussed unreasonable ways of orchestrating a rescue, imagined exerting enough pressure on the hull that the craft began to roll, imagined causing a controlled explosion whose aftershocks might be seen from the surface. We sat, sometimes, as though unintroduced at a dinner party, each waiting for the other to offer their name. On occasion, I would wake from sleeping to find Jelka muttering to herself in the kitchen or the wash stall or the doorway to the main deck and it would take me seconds to get it clear in my head that she was praying.

"Your God," Matteo said to her once, "has put us in a shitty situation." His voice had taken on a tone of disbelief that seemed to follow him about our shared space, a disbelief that stoppered up the other aspects of his personality and made him curt and difficult. "I want," he said a lot, "to eat some normal food. I want a cocktail olive and a pizza and a pack of Melba toasts. I want to stretch my legs. I want to see some fucking weather." I wanted to tell him that of course I felt that way as much as he did, but it seemed unkind, too nagging in a desperate situation. I wanted to tell him that of course I felt afraid, but it seemed too unlucky to say the thing out loud.

I came to regard my role onboard as something akin to peacemaker, although Matteo and Jelka were never exactly fighting, only scratching about one another in a manner I sought to defuse. I tried to fill silences, told stories to drown out the madness of the situation. "Once a month," I said, "when I was little, my father would pack up the Volvo, throw me into the passenger seat, and take me out to the beach. We didn't do much when we were there, we'd just collect pieces of sea glass and cowrie shells. We'd walk the length of the beach, marking our progress via these beach huts that ran along the top of the sands. You could tell how far you'd walked by the color of the beach house you were looking at. The hut painted peach marked the midway point between car park and headland, the hut striped white and blue was the three-quarter point, and so on. When we'd walked far enough, we'd go down to the water and eat sandwiches and look for beached barrel jellyfish. There always seemed to be so many—they're pink when you see them in the water but they always go blue when they wash up on shore. Thing is there's basically nothing to a jellyfish. Almost all of what you picture when you picture a jellyfish is actually just water, this thin skin and then this hood around its reproductive organs and its digestive system. Basically, the second a jellyfish is washed up, it starts to die because the water starts to evaporate. It only takes a few hours in the sun."

"Yes, I know all of that," Jelka interrupted, "but thank you for the biology lesson."

I looked at her, blinked, looked away. It hadn't occurred to me that this was a story I was more used to telling Miri. In my head, I think I'm often telling Miri stories, logging away information or things I've seen in order to tell her about them later. Even trapped as I was down there, I was still doing this: taking everything in with one eye on how to recount it. I think I've trained myself to look at things this way, as if for her as well as for me. Although now, writing this, I'm not sure I really want her to know about it. I can't say whether this is a story I actually want to tell.

The noise had retreated since the first time but returned again, intermittently and then often. It became possible to tell one time period from another, only by virtue of when the noise sounded and when it stopped. Sometimes I would fall asleep in silence and wake to the noise, sometimes vice versa. When it came, it winnowed out around the sides of the craft, creaked like floorboards, like straining rope, like something wrapped around our hull and pressing inward. Sometimes I thought about what it might be but more often I didn't.

Once, I came through to the main deck to find Matteo with his cheek against the window, not looking outward, staring at the floor. When I asked him what he was doing he told me he'd been trying to get cool, gestured to the cheek not touching the window as if inviting me to touch. "I don't feel hot," he said when I asked him, "I just feel weird—you know the feeling right before your leg falls asleep." There was nothing beyond the window, the way there was always nothing. It made me feel restless, anxious to see something move. *This was meant to be a research trip*, I wanted to grumble. *How are we supposed to conduct research on something we can't see?* The water was directionless in its blackness, moving no visible way. It was difficult, particularly if you looked for too long, to imagine there was water around us at all.

We ate a lot of concentrates, drank purified water. There was more of everything than we had expected; at one point I unearthed a bottle of wine in one of the food lockers, though I stowed it away as soon as I found it. *Deceptive, this space*, the woman from the Centre had told us when she showed us around, rapping her knuckles against one of the lockers. *Designed that way. Space efficiency—you'll be shocked how much you can stow.* She had spoken like that about everything, the way you might try to sell someone a car. The lighting, she said, was designed to enhance vitamin D metabolization. The ceilings, she said, were designed to give the greatest possible illusion of space. *Unsinkable*, she said, tapping her toe against the bulkhead and then correcting herself. *I mean, not unsinkable, obviously.*

Time passed. However little happened to hurry it along, it still passed. Days, weeks, I couldn't tell you. We ate and slept and tried the comms panel. Jelka and I did jumping jacks in the rear chamber, kicked our knees up to our chests to get the blood flowing, lay down and bicycled our legs in the air. It felt important, in a dull way, to remain active, important to tidy away after eating, important to remain awake until it became absolutely necessary to sleep again. Sometimes, Matteo would draw a great grid of dots on a piece of paper and convince one of us to play Dots and Boxes. Sometimes, Jelka would sit with her legs up on one of the benches and stare into space for what felt like hours at a stretch. It's insane, of course, that we did so little, insane how little it occurred to us to do. Certainly we were trapped, but in retrospect it's still hard to imagine the kind of lethargy that seemed to grip us. I can't explain it, except to say that inaction felt obvious, a decision already made by someone else. The basic truth of the situation occurred to me only as if shouted across some great distance and barely heard. I felt afraid, of course—but, beneath this, still in some sense quietly removed. I suppose a body has to find a way to cope with panic. I don't know how this works. Panic, as I've said, is a waste of oxygen.

I thought about Miri, sometimes. Tried not to because of the very particular ache it summoned and then did it anyway. I thought about Miri describing the type of cat she'd like to adopt, about Miri brushing her hand over my hair in the way she often did. When I couldn't think about Miri anymore, I gave up and thought instead about the imprints of deliquesced jellyfish, the brown and pink remainders—only imprints—fading to nothing on a white expanse of shore.

MIRI

Years ago, when we were still new, Leah took me out to a bar and then to another bar and then to a late-night movie where we bought popcorn and sat together in the dark. The movie was a '60s thriller: the mutineering crew of a tramp steamer set adrift on a sea of carnivorous seaweed, beset by time-traveling Spanish conquistadors, giant hermit crabs, octopuses, and sharks. Every time another obviously puppeteered monster or oversize plastic snail appeared on-screen, we both shrieked with laughter. *I can't believe you've never seen this movie,* Leah hissed, *it's so terrible. I used to watch it with my dad.* In the dark, I kissed her and she tasted like popcorn. *I think you're perfect,* I said, like an idiot, and she was kind and let me pretend I hadn't said it.

We came back out into the open air around midnight and Leah gave me her coat, pulled me close by the lapels, and then interrupted herself with a laugh before she could kiss me. *People do this in movies,* she said, *but now I just feel daft.* A dribble of fine gold chain around her neck, the chilly flush at the tips of her ears. *You know,* she said, with the portentousness of the evening's many whiskeys, *I love going into the cinema when it's still light and then coming out in the dark. Makes me think about the way a city is never the same. I mean, the way everything changes. Every night, every minute, it's over and things will never be the same again.* I put my hands over her hands, still fisted in the lapels of the coat she had given me, and made her pull me forward. *That makes no sense*, I told her, and she kissed me in the street.

————————

The therapist sends us a bill for the session Leah missed and a note requesting clarity on whether we plan to continue. The Centre, apparently, is willing to bankroll sessions attended but not sessions skipped or rescheduled. Leah is in the bath when I get the invoice, though she has left the door unlocked, which is new. When I come in, she looks up, head back against the lip of the tub, and her skin seems to shrink and then re-shape before me—the stretch and settle of a rubbed eye, briefly off-center, then nothing unusual at all. I sit down on the toilet seat and we regard one another for a moment.

"What are we supposed to do," I say, at last, "about what's happening."

"I don't want a doctor," she says, anticipating my suggesting it again.

"But what if it gets worse?"

"It isn't."

She isn't being unkind, or sharp, or dismissive, not like she has been recently. Her tone is perfectly reasonable, even kind. Beneath it, however, there is little enough in the way of feeling, a chilly blank where the rest of her voice, as I know it, should be. There is nothing of the previous night, when she dipped her head into my shoulder. Something has crested the surface between us and sunk again, the water closing over its head. She moves her hands through the water—the soft and semitranslucent blue at her hip and thigh—and I know she is only talking because I am making her talk.

"I don't know how you can know that," I continue, and she shrugs, a squeeze and pulse of unnatural color around her neck and shoulders, as though water is massing beneath the upper layers of her skin.

"I feel basically OK today," she says, then keeps talking before I can interrupt, "and when I don't, it usually passes."

I look at her, at the way she tries to smile and then seems to give up, ducking beneath the water and holding herself there. I look at her and feel unusually sure that the Leah of the previous night was my Leah, but that this one almost certainly isn't. If I cut her, I'm not altogether sure she would bleed. I feel, at once, a sense of cavernous terror at being left alone and then set it aside. I reach for the plastic vase on the windowsill and ask if she wants me to wash her hair.

—————

When we first moved in together, Toby and Sam helped us with the boxes and afterward sat on the floor and drank wine and ate oven pizzas off mismatched plastic plates. Sam was wearing dungarees, which was odd, as she typically didn't dress that way. Toby had tied a bandanna around his forehead, made a jokingly chivalrous point of carrying the heaviest pieces of furniture. The upstairs neighbors were playing their television loudly—a game show or a nature program, I forget which—and we commented on this only in passing, unaware of what a permanent fixture it would turn out to be. By the time we stopped for pizza, the furniture was mostly in place, though we still had to put the bed together, still had to construct two of the three flat-pack bookcases we had bought in a panic on realizing the flat didn't come furnished as previously described. Toby uncorked a second bottle of wine, told a long story about running into Poppy at the train station, about all the issues she seemed to be having with her boyfriend, Dan. *Something I find incredibly boring*, Sam said, *is everyone's conviction that love is different for them. Somehow harder. Do you know what I mean? I just don't think it's that complicated, honestly—if you're with the wrong person, it's hard. It's just another way of thinking you're special, the way everyone does when they're a teenager. You think you aren't able to love, except that of course you are. You think you aren't able to love correctly or the same as everyone else, except that of course you are, you just haven't had a chance to do it yet. You're not special, you're just waiting.* Toby nodded, poured wine into plastic cups. *In fairness, babe, I don't think Poppy was saying she's unable to love. Just that she hates the way Dan eats with his mouth open.*

Much of the furniture we had was my mother's. She had died three months previously and people were still not past the point of tilting their heads to one side and nodding sympathetically when I said almost anything at all. I had brought a Welsh dresser from my mother's house, a wine rack, a large oval mirror. The latter was a mistake—it seemed to haunt me about the flat as I tried to find a suitable place to put it, appearing at times to reflect not me but my mother's empty house, as though on a time delay. I tapped the second knuckle of a finger lightly against the glass and it sounded like something knocking to be let in.

We had combined our books, our spices, mixed up my table salt with Leah's jars of nutmeg and rosemary and herbes de Provence. We found we had too many table lamps, not enough cutlery. In the chaos of moving our boxes up the stairs, a full set of dishes were smashed. *Do you think,* Toby said over the pizza, *that this is your forever place?* Leah rolled her eyes at him, asked how anything could be your forever place when it was only a rental. *That's true*, Toby said, suddenly narrowing his eyes at Sam, *when are you going to buy us a forever place?* Sam snorted, leaned back on her elbows, and surveyed me upside down. *Haven't I got a bitch of a wife?* she said, and laughed.

Later on, when Toby and Sam had left, we found ourselves too lazy to put the bed together and so stacked sofa cushions on the living room floor, curled up with the new internet contract, which neither of us could make sense of, finishing the second bottle of wine. In the dark, the room was strange-shaped, shadows feeding my anxiety. I imagined us freshly moved into a place where things might walk about at night, where a knock might sound at the door at any moment, where a hand might emerge from behind the curtains to pull either one of us away. *It will be fine, won't it*, I asked in the dark, and Leah locked her ankles around mine.

———

I call the Centre to talk about the therapy bill and find that once again, I can't get through. I put the phone down and think, in a blunt and ugly manner, that I do not have the patience for this. Leah is still in the bath, so I spoon table salt into a glass of water and take it through to her. She seems happy about this, drinks half of it down in a way that makes me feel vaguely nauseated, before pouring the rest into the bath. I leave her be and sit in the spare room, researching skin conditions on my phone, more out of habit than anything, until my battery dies.

———

Getting married was easy—twenty minutes, in and out. When I decided I wanted to get married, I told Leah and she started crying, which I hadn't expected. *I knew you wanted to,* she said, *I'm not surprised, I'm just crying.* Carmen said she was quite startled to know that I'd been the one to do the asking, since I was the one with longer hair. *I didn't mean that the way it came out*, she said, *I meant to say congratulations*, and then she hugged me in a way that moved me a surprising amount. The town hall was having issues with its electrical supply thanks to a workman accidentally running a drill bit through the mains, and so the registrar had lit the room with battery-operated candles, which made everything seem more like a school play than it should have done. *This is good*, Leah said, *mood lighting. People usually have to pay for this sort of thing.* I told her to take it seriously and she smiled at me (the way her face moved, the way I had to tip my head up a little to look at her) and said that she'd never told a joke in her life. In the candle-dark, then, we got married, and came out afterward to gentle rain and no plans for the rest of the day, which felt like a miracle. Leah suggested we find something to eat and walked us over the road to a place that sold burgers, her hand in my hand like something obvious, something grown from the fabric of my own body and pressing out. The afternoon was strange-colored, inconsistent, the way the sky goes dark before a thunderstorm but the grass is still lit up and you can't figure out where the light is coming from.

LEAH

The world was different once, dry, before a century of rain that filled the oceans. Sometimes I think about this, the way that things might once have walked about the deepest places without fear of drowning. Sometimes I think of oceans rising faster than it is possible to escape them, of water drawing tight around the boundaries of the land.

Jelka sat cross-legged on the floor of the main deck, and for whatever reason I imagined her sitting by a campfire. I took a torch and set it down by her feet, crouched down opposite to complete the illusion.

"Now we just need marshmallows to toast," I said, though she only twitched her head—a quick, frustrated gesture, as though I was talking over something she was trying to hear. She was unnervingly still. Beside her, the Saint Brendan figurine stood with his face to the wall.

"It's my birthday," she said, and I looked at her through the upward beam of the torch.

"I didn't know that," I said. I didn't ask how she could possibly know this either, with no way of recording the time or date, no way of knowing how long we'd been here. "We should do something to celebrate." She nodded and didn't say anything further. I could hear Matteo knocking about in the rear chamber, kicking his feet against the benches. He had been growing increasingly irritable, prone to interrupting his own sentences to ask if we could hear a noise, complaining it was preventing him from thinking clearly. I would hear him moving about when I was trying to sleep, and think about my neighbors—mine and Miri's—and the television they never switched off. Once, I woke to find him standing at the foot of my bunk, though when I asked him what he was doing he apologized quite genuinely and told me he must have drifted off.

"I can smell it again," Jelka said now, gazing in a seemingly untroubled fashion into the torch beam. She was talking about the usual smell, the suppurating meat smell that had saturated all of our clothes by this point, though we washed and wrung them under the shower spray and hung them out across the benches to dry. I said nothing and Jelka continued, "I wonder if it's actually just us, you know. The smell. I wonder if this is how people smell, this far down."

I thought of reminding her that we'd both noticed the smell the first time when we were still descending but found I didn't have the energy to argue.

"And what about that sound," she said then. "What about the talking, the words. Can you hear that?"

There was nothing, not just then—there had never been any talking—and I couldn't picture what it was she was imagining or think of a useful thing to say. Instead, I only commanded her to make a wish, the way one would on a collection of birthday candles, and then to blow on the torch beam, which she did until I switched it off.

———

I want whoever reads this to understand what they're getting, which is mainly confusion, because I don't know how to be clear about any of this.

In the dark, I pressed my face against the main-deck window

and saw nothing. The blackness seemed another color, something less than black, altogether more devoid, more dumbfounding. I thought again about falling, imagined us tight in the grip of something that had snatched us down to the place we were already going, and then lifted my cheek from the glass and realized I didn't know how I had come to be here. I had, it appeared, been sleeping, and now I was here.

"You, too?" Matteo said, and I turned and found him standing in the doorway from the rear chamber, silhouetted wide and rolling his knuckles down along the side of his face.

"I wasn't here," I said, hearing the illogic of what I had said a moment after I said it, though Matteo only nodded, crossing to sit at the comms panel and look at me baldly.

"I know, buddy," he said, and then, "d'you ever think about how we had a plan—that there were things we were supposed to be doing down here?"

I blinked at him, tried to pull to the fore of my mind an image of the Centre, the research project we had prepped for, the concept of something intended and carried out. I looked back toward the main console, the dim lights and the small carved insignia on the top of the panel: the dark squinting eye etched in metal. Matteo watched me for several seconds before leaning back in his chair and nodding.

"I know, it bothers me, too. The way I don't think."

I tried to shake my head, to tell him that wasn't what was happening. Phantom fingers at the base of my skull, moving downward: *sunken thoughts.* Who had said that? I remembered, but it took me longer than it should have done to dredge the name from the bottom of my mind.

MIRI

Things continue. This is something I have always found: unfortunately, things go on.

Leah bathes for approximately sixty percent of the day, though this is swiftly becoming something more like seventy. I go out and come back again, I do my work and fail to do my work and watch movies that I can't follow and that fail to drown out the noise of the neighbors' TV. When Leah is out of the bath, I try to make her eat, though this is largely unsuccessful. Her appetite, already poor, seems to be dwindling further. I bring her salt dissolved in beakers of water, and this seems to stave off the hard recurring pulse in her neck and shoulders that always sees her back in the bath again before much time has passed. For how little she eats, she doesn't seem to be bearing up too badly, though "badly" is a relative term these days. There is something hanging over us that I seem to feel most clearly in the mornings, before the haze of my new routine has descended, before I have seen her into the bath and out of it, before I have lifted her arms to soap as gently as possible at the silvering translucent skin underneath.

Sometimes, when I look in the mirror that has hung in the hall since we moved in, I think I see myself not where I am but back in my mother's house, though this is simply a trick of the light. I don't feel particularly tired, but nor do I feel particularly anything. Even my bad tooth has stopped giving me grief.

The therapist contacts me to ask about a check she received

from the Centre to cover the sessions we have attended so far. It bounced, she says and asks if I have a secondary method of payment. She tells me that she won't be able to continue until we send her the money but suggests that if we need to contact her in an emergency, something could probably be worked out. I call the Centre once I have managed to get her off the phone, though they seem once again to have gone off-grid. The phone no longer clicks onto an automated message after a certain number of rings; now it simply rings on and on until I set the receiver back down.

For the first time since Leah returned, I go to search for the site run by the wives of fictional spacemen, but it has been over three months and I find I cannot recall the address. I google the Centre instead and find that the website I was expecting is likewise not there, only a 404 error message and a suggestion that I check the address before trying again. I shut my laptop and move to make a cup of tea. It occurs to me that I ought to just try visiting the Centre. I've been only once before— picked Leah up on her return—but now I have misplaced the address. I spend an hour going through papers in vain hopes of finding it and then give up. What, after all, am I hoping to say if I get there: *Can you fix her? Can you give her back again, but better?* I imagine ordering a cab and simply asking it to drive around until it comes upon somewhere I recognize. Later on, I will move through the flat, feeling suddenly terrified that each room might cease to exist the moment I leave it. The world is folding over like a book whose past pages I cannot access. I dial the Centre and listen to the phone ring out.

One afternoon, I am subject to a sudden attack of motivation and insist that Leah come with me on a walk. She doesn't want to go, but she has been in the bath all day and the drain is clogged with the scum of whatever it is she leaves behind, so I lay out clothes for her and tell her it will help. She moves oddly now, a certain keel to the left, as though a piece of her is somehow unsupported. I wrap her up and tell her she'll enjoy it.

The year has turned, the days growing shorter, a fact I seem almost entirely to have missed. I take Leah's arm and she doesn't resist me, allows me to tow her up the hill toward a place we used to walk. There is a wide stretch of common land between the circle of flats and houses that border ours, grass uninterrupted by the canals that ring so much of the city. We used to walk here a lot when we first moved, Leah desperate for some space and some air between trips while I was simply happy to accompany her. *Look at that*, she would say, pointing at nothing—a child flying a kite in the shape of a kestrel, a woman loudly breaking up with a man on a bench by the road. Today, she is quiet, goes where I lead her until suddenly seeming to become unable, dragging downward on my arm in a slow-motion movement that it takes me too long to realize is a fall. She goes down where she is on the grass and I don't know what to do or how to get her back to the flat again. A woman, passing by with a dachshund wrapped up in a fuchsia jacket, pauses to ask if my friend is all right and I tell her yes without knowing what I'm saying, let her go without knowing how to ask for her help. Leah lies on the grass where she has fallen, curved into herself like a conch, like something from which a creature might emerge.

I get her home again; I couldn't say how, it just happens. As I said before, things go on. I get her into the bath and keep her there until, by degrees, she seems to feel better, and eventually I manhandle the television into the bathroom, balance it on the toilet seat and plug it into a long extension cord I have rolled in from the bedroom. I put on *Jaws* and ask her to watch it with me, sit on the mat beside the bath and keep one hand on the side of the tub so she can touch me, if she wants to. I think about the first time we watched this movie together, the way she cut herself off in the middle of talking about sharks and told me she didn't want to be boring. She says nothing now, though she seems to follow the movie, flicks water at the back of my head the first time the shark appears. I feel exhausted, a feeling of catching up, a feeling of something finding me. My heart is a thin thing, these days—shred of paper blown between the spaces in my ribs.

LEAH

Jelka on the floor with her ear against the escape hatch, saying something I could not hear. When I asked her what she was doing, she looked up at me, her expression dim in the hard fluorescent light.

"Ghosts don't speak," she said to me. "People misunderstand this. They think that when you're haunted you hear someone speaking but you don't. Or not usually. Most of the time, if you hear something speaking, it's not a ghost—it's something worse."

Her face was not its normal color; it had the look of something sunk in milk. She lowered her ear to the escape hatch again, closed her eyes as if in concentration. "My priest used to say that," she continued, though I hadn't asked for an explanation, "my last priest, before I stopped going. When I was eighteen, I thought I saw a ghost in my mother's house. It was just under the stairs—the place we used to keep shoes—not someone I knew, just someone. It was the middle of the night and it told me it needed help, that it wanted to speak to me. But when I told my priest, he said that it couldn't have been a ghost because a ghost wouldn't have spoken. He said that demons masquerade as ghosts to try to tempt us, to drag us into sinning. You're not supposed to speak to the dead," she added, "it's somewhere in Deuteronomy. *There shall not be found among you any one who burns his son or his daughter as an offering, any one who practices divination, a soothsayer, or an augur, or a sorcerer, or a charmer, or a medium, or a wizard, or a necromancer. For whoever does these things is an abomination to the Lord.* It means you've stopped trusting in God, that you're trying to bypass Him, to bypass His plan. A ghost that speaks is just a demon, trying to tempt you into making that mistake."

I said nothing, only sitting down beside her by the hatch and touching her arm very gently. She hadn't eaten, it occurred to me, in however long. Matteo was somewhere else, presumably on the main deck, though I wasn't aware of this as fact, just as something that had to be. I had woken this way, to Jelka talking in a way I couldn't understand, to the press of electric light and the certainty of darkness without. Jelka didn't respond to my touch, only pressed her ear closer to the hatch. "So what is that," she said, "if it isn't a ghost—*what is it?*"

I looked at her, took my hand away from her arm and looked down at the hatch. I could hear nothing, not even the sound that so frequently ringed itself around us, not even the sound of the ocean, not even Matteo, wherever he might be. There was no sound at all, in fact, except for Jelka talking, asking aloud what it was, what I thought was talking to her through the hatch.

―――――――

When my father died, I was in the other room. He hadn't been ill—or rather, he had but not in a way that seemed threatening. A long and aggravating cough, an occasional breathlessness. I was nineteen and I saw him a lot in the weeks immediately following his death: at the end of my bed, twice in the garden at my mum's house, though at that point they hadn't been on speaking terms for several years. My mum was actually pretty good about it when I told her. *I think seeing things is fine, my love*, she said to me, *I think seeing the things you want is completely natural*. She hugged me a lot during that time and I was grateful for it, though we both knew I had always been closer to my father. It is strange, in a way, to think how much better our relationship became in his absence. When she died, ten years later, I cried harder than I had over my father and felt the drag of her loss in a fiercer and somehow more desperate way. It surprised me, the ache of my missing her and how long it lasted. I didn't see her afterward the way I had seen my father. Once gone, my mum stayed gone. I didn't tell anyone about seeing my father, except for my mum and, much later, Miri. I don't know anything about ghosts, except that I guess I've seen one, which makes me believe that other people probably have, too. When I told her about it, the first time, Miri widened her eyes at me and said, *I thought you were a scientist*, adding that she didn't believe in ghosts, in a manner that should have been rude but actually wasn't. *I mean I'm jealous*, she said, *I suppose. When I was a kid I really wanted to believe in that sort of thing*.

When my father died, I inherited most of his possessions and sold a lot of them. I kept the things that already felt like mine: the books and the diving almanac, the boxes of magazines and the good, big coat that he always let me borrow when we walked on the beach. I saw him many times in the direct aftermath of his death, waved whenever he appeared and never felt compelled to speak to him. There was really no unfinished business, which I think is what stopped that whole thing being frightening—that and the fact that, ghost or not, it was still only ever my father. There was no sense of *haunting*, to be honest, only ongoingness, until one day he ceased to appear and I really felt fine about that, too.

MIRI

The phone rings at midnight and I do not answer it. Leah is in the bath and I am in the bathroom with her. The sound machine is playing its usual noises and for the first time I don't register it as an imposition, so much as a constant element of the space we share. The phone rings again at one and we are in the same position. I've been reading to Leah from a book she bought me once and ignoring the way she moves her hands through the water, ignoring the thought of the way a body moves when it's been broken, the backward drift and slip of something functioning incorrectly.

"Did you know," she says at one point—the dreaming lecture-voice that tells me she has, for the moment, forgotten me—"did you know that we all carry the ocean in our bodies, just a little bit? Blood is basically made up of sodium, potassium, calcium—more or less the same as seawater, when you really get down to it. The first things came from the sea, of course, so there's always going to be a little trace of it in everything, a little trace of salt in the bones."

Shortly after this, I ask her if she wants to come to bed. "You've been soaking all day," I tell her and she nods and tells me that ideally, she'd like a little bit longer. "The water's cold," I say and she tells me that's fine and I think, in a peculiar way, of how similar this is to before, despite everything—the way that Leah was so often fine when I wasn't, the way that I seemed so endlessly clenched and tense and prone to discomfort where Leah was simply happy to sit as she was. *The reason you get heartburn*, she used to say, *is because you're letting your whole body squeeze you too tight.* She would sit me down on the sofa and hold a hand to my rib cage, mime the breaking of a grip as though someone had clenched a fist around my lungs and was wringing them.

"I still think you should come to bed," I tell her, but she shakes her head peaceably and turns her attention back to the water. I'm not sure why I press the matter, except to say that it seems easier, in the dark, with the sound machine playing over the tops of my words, to speak and imagine the things I say might land. "I'd really like you to come to bed," I say, and when she doesn't respond I take her hand and try to pull it, "just for a bit," I say, and I don't know why I'm angry and I don't know what it is that I want or why I pull so hard that she half stands in the bath. "I don't want to," she says and I tell her I think this is silly, that it's all so silly. "I don't want to," she tells me again, and I'm trying to heave her out of the bath and then she is leaking water from the beds of her eyes, from the insides of her ears, from the side of her mouth, and her legs are not supporting her and my skin is screaming and I catch her beneath the arms to stop her falling and to stop this moment from being my fault.

There was a test I could have taken, you know, that would have told me whether or not I'm likely to develop the same condition as my mother. I never took it, though I meant to. The sharp end of a day and Leah asking if I thought I would do it—*for your own peace of mind,* she had said, and then, *but only if you think it will matter.* I had gone out one day with the purpose of sorting it, had booked a test and walked through town in a thin and drifting rain that settled like a layer of fabric across my shoulders and back. I had reached the place where the test was due to be carried out fifteen minutes early and, thinking vaguely that it would do to while away the time before my appointment, had simply turned around and walked home again. I'd been back on my sofa watching television several hours before I realized what I'd done.

I suppose I think about this sometimes; the reason for booking a test and the reason for missing it. It is easier, I guess, to believe that life is inexhaustible. Not so much that its opportunities are vast or that one's personal dreams can be reached at any age or season, but rather to believe that every dull or daily thing you do will happen again any number of times over. To stamp a limit on even the most tedious of things—the number of times you have left to buy a coffee, the number of times you will defrost the fridge—is to acknowledge reality in a way that amounts to torture. In truth, we will only perform any action a certain number of times, and to know that can never be helpful. There is, in my opinion, no use in demanding to know the number, in demanding to know upon waking the number of boxes to be ticked off every single day. After all, why would it help to be shown the mathematics of things, when instead we could simply imagine that whatever time we have is limitless.

———

The phone rings again at 6 A.M. I have left Leah in the bath, the way she asked me to when her mouth drained of water sufficiently to allow her to talk. I answer the phone and the caller identifies herself as the sister of Jelka, who was on the craft with Leah when it went down. "I'd love to speak," she says, "if that wouldn't be too much trouble. There are some things I think we ought to discuss."

LEAH

Things broke down—I think that's fair to say. Not that this happened suddenly, but my recognition of what was happening still came on in the sudden way things tend to in a crisis. Things were bad, but fine, and then they weren't fine and I'd missed some crucial point by which to fix them. We were trapped, and Jelka was suddenly hearing things that Matteo and I couldn't hear, and there was nothing I could think of to do that didn't involve first rising to the surface and then looking around for help.

Jelka on the main deck, with her cheek against the window. Jelka in the rear chamber, leaning down toward the hatch. Matteo pulling her away, at first with concern but increasingly with something more like impatience. "You're giving me the creeps," he said.

The shower running in the wash stall and no one using it. I turned it off, told them to be more careful, though both claimed not to have left it on.

The noise sometimes waking me, sometimes coming when I was already awake. I held my hands before my face and counted fingers, recollected dreams I'd had at seventeen, of webbing growing down past the knuckle and gill slits in my neck.

Jelka standing with her back to me, looking out toward the dark. The main deck lit by torches lined up along the central console.

The feeling in my legs after I fell asleep and woke again— like pins and needles.

Matteo flinging a plate against the wall and then apologizing for it.

"Let's talk about this, reasonably," I said, then found myself unable to continue.

Jelka's figure of Saint Brendan turning up in strange places: in the shower tray, in the chest fridge, standing guard beneath my bunk. "I hate that fucking thing," Matteo said, "feels like it's watching me."

I ate something from the stores and wondered how much could possibly be left, wondered why it hadn't started running out yet.

I went into my pack and found the postcard Miri had bought me, the image of a tangerine-colored octopus. PAMELA—GIANT PACIFIC OCTOPUS—ESTIMATED AGE BETWEEN 3 AND 4 YEARS OLD.

"Who are you again?" Matteo said, when I came to join him at the table. "Only kidding," he said, but then asked me why it was we were here.

"I won't speak to you," Jelka's voice in the dark, in her bunk with the blanket thrown up over her head. "This isn't me speaking to you now."

I sat on the main deck and thought again about Sylvia Earle, about something she had said in an article I'd cut out and treasured. Our understanding of the universe, so she said, comes from the ocean: *It has taught us that life exists everywhere, even in the greatest depths; that most of life is in the oceans; and that oceans govern climate. Perhaps because we're so terrestrialy biased, air-breathing creatures that we are, it has taken us until now to realize that everything we care about is anchored in the ocean.* I had my back to the window as I thought this and found myself suddenly unable to bear the oppressive blank of space beyond the glass. *Where are you all*, I wanted to scream, overcome with a sudden vivid grief at the thought of this nothing—no strange deep-ocean creatures, no bioluminescence, no life. *Come on*, I found myself thinking, *give.*

I chewed my tongue to keep from talking and listened to the noise outside the craft.

Matteo dragged Jelka up by her arm, up and away from the hatch where she had been crouching. "I'm *sick* of this," he said, and she pulled her arm away too hard and overbalanced, grabbed the air and fell. "I can't take any more of this fucking *behavior*," he snapped and reeled back as if to kick her, and I pushed myself between them, pushed him away, and he pushed me back and I thought *help*, once, sharply, and wanted Miri even though she was smaller than me.

"I'm sorry," he said to me later, holding his frostbitten hand out to take my elbow, passing his other hand over his face. "I'm sorry, buddy, I'm so fucking sorry, I don't know what's going on." I shook my head at him, wanted to hug him but couldn't quite remember how. Jelka was back where she had been, by the hatch with her head pressed downward, and it seemed easy enough to imagine that nothing had happened at all.

———

There's a point between the sea and the air that is both and also not quite either. Does that make sense? I'm talking about the point at the very top of the ocean that is constantly evaporating and condensing, where water yearns toward air and air yearns toward water. I think about this sometimes, that middle place, the struggle of one thing twisting into another and back again.

I was asleep, which is why I missed what happened. I woke to Jelka screaming and Matteo seeming both to be pushing her up and pushing her away from him. He told her she was fucking crazy, repeated it and repeated it and she fell down and started sobbing and I wasn't sure what was going on, so couldn't really do anything except push myself between them again and hope things would start to make sense. Matteo wouldn't explain, only told me he couldn't be where he was and crashed away to the main deck, leaving me with Jelka. I asked her what had happened but she refused to speak to me, remaining where she was on the floor of the rear chamber, pressing her head down toward the escape hatch, grinding her forehead into the metal. I sat down beside her and I thought about everything I had hoped to do, the things I had wanted to study and see and the trappedness of everything, the darkness, the lack. *This isn't the ocean*, I thought to myself, once and very clearly, *I just wanted to see the ocean*, and then for a long time after that I thought nothing because I realized it would be easier.

"I was trying to make him listen," Jelka said, after a very

long time of saying nothing, and I nodded, as though this was what I had expected her to say. "I know I shouldn't be listening," she said, "I know I'm not supposed to respond, but I can't stop it now. I hear it all the time. I thought if he would listen with me, it would make it easier. Do you hear it, Leah? The voice—whatever it is—do you hear it?"

She was looking at me now, sitting up and gripping my arm, and I could see the shape of her jawbone, like something I could remove from the rest of her skull with only a minimum of effort.

"I don't," I told her, helplessly, "because there's nothing to hear."

Much later, I left Jelka in her bunk and went through to the main deck, where I found Matteo sitting in a circle of torches. "I read a story once," he told me, "about a paranormal detective who spent a night in a haunted room, and as long as he was inside this ring he'd created, this ring of protective objects, nothing could get at him." I asked him if I could come inside the circle and he shook his head at me. "Nothing personal, buddy," he said and looked like he meant it. "I'd just rather you didn't, right now."

The sound was back, the surging and retreating, a whirring, whistling, rending sound that I knew wasn't all that Jelka heard.

"What do you think it is we're here for," Matteo asked me, and I looked at him inside his circle and felt unsure of what to say.

"I don't think they told us the truth," he said when I didn't answer him, and I shrugged and looked toward the windows, the way I often did, listening to the sound as it whaled itself around the craft and trying to imagine what it was Jelka could hear speaking in its place. "I mean," Matteo said, "we both know this, don't we? They shipped us off with so much food onboard. The comms went out before the system died, like they switched us off externally. We know all this, we *know* this."

I nodded, shrugged again, tried to imagine how I would have felt when I was used to feeling anything. I thought about Pamela, wondered if I would still remember her name if I didn't have a postcard to remind me. I thought of the upward curl of her arms, the way she boiled up out of the water to reach for me. I thought of the shock of her strength, the first time, the way she had gripped me from right wrist to elbow as one of the keepers pulled at my shoulder and told me I'd just made a friend.

"I feel like we're waiting for something," Matteo continued, "or experimenting with something. I don't feel like this is a research trip. Don't you think? Feels more like being dropped in a tank at feeding time and waiting for the sharks to come out."

I nodded, understanding what he was saying but somehow unable to get my mind off the octopus, the tight but forgiving press of a creature strong enough to break my bones and yet choosing not to.

"They said it was a research trip," said Matteo. "Do you remember that? Because sometimes I feel like I don't, like I'm forgetting."

"I don't think it's that important," I said, but didn't mean that so much as that there were other things, more important things, that I felt in danger of forgetting.

"She's hearing things that aren't there," he said, after a pause. "I don't know what to do about it."

"Neither do I," I said, and after that I went to sleep for a long time on the floor next to Matteo's circle of torches. I dreamed in pieces, shapes and shards of broken pictures: I dreamed about the octopus, knew her name and then forgot it, and I dreamed about Miri, except her face was different and something was off about the way she moved, on all fours rather than upright, and not toward me but somehow to the side. And I dreamed that it *was* the ocean after all, that I was in the ocean, but not the ocean as I knew it. I dreamed that it was a different part, something older and deeper, and I dreamed that there were things there with me, in the dark.

MIRI

The woman across from me is tall in a way I'm not used to and worries at the skin of her upper lip so hard that at one point during our conversation she has to pause to press a paper napkin to the center of her mouth.

"I'm so sorry," she says, "it's a disgusting habit," and I nod and hand over my own napkin because I've done this to myself so many times before. We're in the café I often visit with Carmen and I wonder in a way that passes in and out of my mind like a flickering light how long it's been since I last checked in with Carmen.

"Do people keep trying to bring you coffee?" the woman across from me asks, when she returns from the counter bearing two cups of tea and a slice of depressed-looking apple cake. "I don't know. Maybe that's just my experience. When I told people what had happened, at the beginning, everyone just seemed to want to keep me extremely well caffeinated all the time, as if I would want to be particularly awake for all of this, you know?"

Her voice is oddly formal, with an accent I cannot quite place, and it occurs to me that she must look similar to Jelka, except that I cannot for the life of me remember what it was that Jelka looked like. We met once, of course, at the reception the Centre held before they left, but I remember little of her and can only impose the image of this stranger over the top. Her name is Juna, something she has to tell me twice and pronounces with a

J that bends into the shape of a *Y*. She is taller than me, better kept, blue veins forking at her wrists like roots, and she is my age, I think, or slightly older, though various things about her make it difficult to be sure.

"*Six extra shots*, my friend used to say," and she is talking to me still, rolling her eyes up in a way that seems at once friendly and impersonal, as if this is a story she would just as happily tell in the office. "He'd bring me these enormous coffees, these buckets of the stuff, and I'd think to myself, *Six extra shots and I'll be on the ceiling*. I shouldn't complain though, I know," she adds and hitches up one sleeve and then the other with an odd, precise gesture that is not at all interesting except I have never met a person who moves in exactly this way. "Having people be kind to you is so important, but it's also incredibly irritating. It's hard to find the balance of what you're actually able to accept without wanting to hit someone."

I nod, sip my tea, and wonder what it is I'm doing here. I hadn't been keen on leaving Leah, had half considered calling Sam to come and watch her while I was gone, before thinking that of course I couldn't, that there was somehow no way of bringing a third party into the situation at this late stage. Instead, I had left Leah in the bath with the TV on but as far away from the water as possible, turned her sound machine on to its middle setting, and told her I would be back as soon as I could. I had almost abandoned the plan of meeting Jelka's sister, telling myself several times even as I dressed that morning and even as I put on my shoes to leave that I ought to call and cancel, that I was in fact just about to do so, that that was the very next thing I would do.

"Thank you for the tea," I say now, mainly for the sake of

saying something, and Juna nods at me, takes a forkful of apple cake, and pulls a face.

"This is horrible," she says, and continues to eat it, which amuses me enough to make me sit up a little. "I'm very happy you agreed to meet me," she adds, curiously formal again, gummed with apple cake. "I know how things can be."

"It's OK," I say, and she nods, looks at me frankly for a moment.

"I'm sorry I called so early," she says. "When I called you, I mean, I called early. I didn't plan to, but I wasn't sleeping well and I took a chance that you weren't either. I thought it would be good to speak," she says, though she has already said this several times, on the phone and then again when I first arrived at the café and found her waiting there. "My sister and your wife—" she says. "Do you say *wife*, actually? I'm sorry, I wasn't sure."

I'm bewildered by this, nod, and she adjusts her sleeves again. "OK," she says. "My sister and your wife were on the dive together, as you know."

"I know, we met," I say. "Your sister and me. Just once, at the party before they went away. I don't think you were there."

I'm not sure if this is an interruption, though she doesn't behave as if it is. She nods her head, cracks the knuckle of her index finger beneath her thumb in a gesture that seems somehow conversational.

"I've been putting off getting in touch with you for a long time," she says, "and I wasn't even sure how to reach you at first or what it was I was supposed to say. I've been doing a lot of saying the wrong thing, recently, and I'm trying not to do that so much—"

"Did you call me all those other times?" I ask, and this is definitely an interruption—sharp tines of her fork coming down on the table. "Someone's been calling me at weird hours," I say. "They never answer when I pick up the phone, though I don't always pick up the phone anymore."

"No," she says, not unkindly. "I called you once, and you answered me."

I look at her, focus in close on her collarbones, on the bright coral beads at her neck. She has the look of someone correctly joined together, well-oiled, unlikely to collapse. When I interrupt, she doesn't raise an eyebrow, only crosses one leg over the other and nods into the moment. She is someone who eats the disappointing cake she has ordered for herself, someone who allows me to throw the conversation off its hinge.

"I had some calls," I say. "I've been having them forever, like before Leah came back, even—and I thought they were from the Centre but now I just don't know. Did you see their website's disappeared?"

I don't know why I'm talking like this. It's been a while since I spoke to anyone who wasn't Leah, a while since I did anything but sit by the bath watching television, and soft-boil eggs, and stir salt into glasses of tap water. Across the table, Juna is still nodding, tilts her head one way and then the other in a manner that may be understanding or may simply be an effort to work out a kink.

"Yes, I saw that, too," she says, "I'd been expecting it. I've been trying to talk to some people, you see, looking into some things. I think I know what the phone calls you've been getting might have been about, but really, I think it's best if you let me go from the beginning."

Her skin, I notice, is foundation-smeared to an optical illusion of smoothness that, on closer inspection, only thinly
covers its pits and scars. I understand the formality of her ges-
tures a little more in relation to this, the way she pulls her
sleeves away from her wrists to prevent unintentionally stain-
ing the fabric with makeup, the way she tilts her chin upward
every fifteen seconds as though remembering to keep her skin
away from her collar. I am still considering her skin when she
speaks again, and the meaning of her words takes a moment
to sink in.

"I need to tell you that my sister is dead," she says, "and I
need to tell you what I know."

My face feels stiff, as though I've washed it with hand soap, and the
tooth that has sat curiously dormant at the back of my jaw
for however long has spontaneously resumed aching. I am
in the kitchen, and Leah is in the bathroom, and I don't
know how long I've been here or how long it's been since
I returned home, but the sunlight is peeling away from the
kitchen worktops like paper torn in strips. I let Juna speak
for a while and then told her I'd had enough, but that maybe
she could phone me, at some other time, on some other day,
and then I left without paying for my tea and had to double
back when I realized. *It's fine*, Juna said when I almost ran
into her outside the café, *I've paid for it. Least I can do.* And
then she walked me part of the way home while telling me a
very long and frankly incomprehensible story about an older
couple she knew who appeared to have had polyamorous af-
fairs with half of the people she knew in the city. *You know*

when two people are fifty, she said, *and not at all interesting but somehow their open marriage has consumed the lives of everyone around them? I'm sorry, I don't know why I'm telling you this story. I think I'm just trying to make noise.*

Now, in the kitchen, I appear to have made myself another cup of tea despite having had one at the café. Leah's sound machine is making a strange, juddering noise, as though something has come loose in its inner machinery and is causing the usual noise to sound arrhythmic and somehow off-center. I stand with my back to the counter and sip at the tea I do not want and try to play back everything Juna said to me. *I didn't want to tell you over the phone,* she said several times, *I thought seeing your face would make it easier. Or maybe your seeing my face would make it easier, I don't know.* Her sister was dead, she told me, and the Centre had at first given her contradictory information, then seemed to start screening her calls, then appeared to close up shop altogether. She had been forced to find things out for herself, she told me, had things she needed to show me. I cut her off when I should have allowed her to talk for longer and she told me she understood. *I didn't want you to be alone, trite as that sounds,* she said. *We can talk again, if you would like to.*

I think about all of this now with a peculiarly glassy sensation, as though I might raise my hand to my face and find it made of some hardened material, as though my thoughts might turn out to be equally so. I am thinking about all of this when the sound machine abruptly shuts off in the next room and Leah makes a sound halfway between a cry and loud exhalation and I realize she is standing in the doorway to the hall, naked and still wet, and that one of her eyes is no longer an eye but a strange, semisolid globe that on closer inspection appears to be made up of pure water. When it bursts, it falls down her face like a yolk escaping a white and I put a hand over my mouth and nose as though anticipating a smell.

Hadal Zone

LEAH

I don't know how long the next bit took, so let's call it three days. I woke to Saint Brendan at the foot of my bunk—not on the floor but actually in among the covers. When I sat up to ask Jelka why she had done this, I found she was not in the rear chamber with me and shortly afterward Matteo came through from the main deck to say that she was not there either. We found her in the wash stall, under the showerhead in her clothes with her face turned upward, mouth open to drink the water. "What are you doing," Matteo asked her, in a voice that did not seem to expect a response.

I brought her out of the wash stall and sat her on my bunk in her wet clothes. She seemed sharp beneath my hands. I wanted to push her hair around, pull it away from her face. *What are you doing*, I wanted to ask her.

"I'm tired of hearing it," she said to me then, grasped my wrist and looked at me the way people do when they're drunk and about to tell you a secret. (Miri leaning toward me across the table in a bar—our third or fourth date—a sweet slur, *I've been thinking about you, a bit. I bite the tips of my fingers and I think about you.*) "I'm tired of hearing it," Jelka said, "and I don't hear it so badly when I'm in there."

I let her hold my wrist and look at me as if she was willing me to understand. "You know what I mean, don't you?" she said. "I know you'd have to hear it, a little bit—if you tried.

The big sound, like the ocean, that's just a distraction. There's something else, if you listen properly, if you try—"

And then Matteo ruined everything by pushing me aside and slapping her right across the face—and that was the first day.

The second day was the second day because at some point I woke up to it. I jogged several laps around the rear chamber the way I had taken to doing to prevent my legs from shaking when I stood up too fast. It was back by then, the whaling sound, the familiar curling, *oom*ing, and I thought about what Jelka had said about it being a distraction from something else. I did not listen, closed my eyes, and jogged in circles around the space I knew by heart. I ate something from the chest freezer, I thought about Miri, and I went through to the main deck, where I found Matteo sitting in his circle of torches and a panel on one of the main control boards smashed across its center, three buttons cracked, as though they had been hit with some force. One of the torches in Matteo's circle, I noticed, was also cracked across its reflector, but I found I was too tired to comment on any of this, so I only sat with my back against the comms panel and looked toward the window until he started to speak.

"Did you ever think that maybe this is just a dead part," he said, after a moment. "I mean, not that we're not in the ocean but that we've somehow fallen down into some part of it that died however many years ago and now there's nothing here at all."

I didn't look at him, kept my eyes trained on the window. (Miri placing her hands on either side of my face to shake me when I drifted away from the thread of a conversation. *Are you there? Or is this person a replicant?*)

"When I went ice fishing with my dad," Matteo said, hold-ing up his hand with its missing fingers as if to remind me, "it was so still and bleak—temperatures below freezing, of course—but you still knew there was life down there, just un-der the ice. When you cut a hole, baited the hook, you were already anticipating the frenzy, the thing below that was ready to fight you when you tried to pull it up. This doesn't feel like that," he said, and I wanted to tell him that I disagreed, that I felt certain we were still somewhere where something else ex-isted alongside us, that there had to be something here that we simply couldn't see. I felt, as I often did, an agony at the empti-ness, of wanting to see where we were and assess it for myself, but I didn't know how to say that without sounding like Jelka. I stared out of the window, willing something to blink back at me, and then I closed my eyes and thought about the book about the *Trieste* and the Challenger Deep that I had borrowed so often from my father: its turquoise cover, talismanic in the fact that it was the same color as my lunch box, the same color as the toothpaste my mother used, the same color as the single fleck in my father's right eye.

When I came back through to the rear chamber sometime later, Jelka had once again been in the wash stall and I found her wet and clothed and leaning up against the table, staring at the floor. I didn't ask her what she was doing, only moved to-ward the worktop to make a cup of tea. I felt, rather than saw, her reach out for me and dodged her, drew back my elbow and edged toward the sink. At that moment, I felt unable to toler-ate the thought of her asking me once again if I heard some noise I couldn't hear. I feel bad about that now. Of everything, this is the thing that makes me feel worst.

The third day came in two parts, which I will call morning

and evening, though there was little enough to differentiate them beyond what will shortly become obvious. I did my jog around the rear chamber and then found something to eat, trying my best to keep my mind along lines that did not seem calculated to hurt it. I had been recollecting a lot of things in Miri's voice, just recently, my memory throwing up some snippet of conversation and then refusing to fill in the blanks (all Miri, all things she had said in the past that my brain had held on to without any obvious reason: *I don't think that kind of thing necessarily makes a person* smarter / *problem is I think I've been trained to think of Catholicism as a sort of winnable game, like a computer game* / *the ubiquity of a straight woman reading an e e cummings poem at a wedding*). Jogging kept my mind temporarily clear, and so I did it, sometimes for what seemed to be hours simply running in circles in my bare feet and uniform. My father had always told me it was better to keep busy, that there could always be something to do if I looked for it. *Things didn't crawl from the sea for the very first time*, he had joked, *for you to pay them back loafing around idle.*

I remember a sensation of damp—a wet pressure along the surface of my skin like the imprint of a finger dipped in water. A directionless quality to everything, though nothing moved except me, in circles. At some point, Matteo came through from the main deck, rubbing his eyes and telling me he'd dreamed the comms panel came online while he was sleeping. "They were all there," he said, and did not offer to explain who he meant. "It came online and they were all still there." It was at this point that the door to the wash stall opened and Jelka emerged, advancing on him quickly. Once again, she was fully clothed and wet from the shower, and she placed her hands on either side of his head, pushing him back against the table so he yelled.

"I told you to listen," she said, and sounded extremely measured, all things considered. "I just want you to listen like I told you."

She was holding his face so tightly that I could see the skin turning white beneath her fingers. He grunted, pushed back against her but seemed unable to dislodge her, bending back against the table as she held on to his head.

"I can't stop it now," she said. "It's all I can hear anymore. I know I'm not supposed to respond but I can't help it. It's like there's something on the inside"—she pressed her thumbs upward into his temples—"like water condensed on the inside of my brain and I can't wipe it away. Ghosts don't speak," she said, again, the way she had before, "but something is speaking to me."

I don't remember what Matteo's face did at that moment; all I remember is her hands and the white of his skin as her fingers crept in toward the corners of his eyes.

"I'm sorry," he said, "I'm sorry. I'll pray if you want me to."

She said nothing to this, only paused for a long time before releasing him, looking at him with an expression that could have meant anything but which I took as proof that Matteo had said the right thing.

"Listen," I said, "why don't I make us some coffee," and things must have been all right for a while after that because the next thing I remember, Jelka was asleep in her bunk and Matteo was eating at the table as though nothing had happened.

"It'll be all right now," I remember Matteo saying, and I didn't ask him what he was basing that on, although oddly enough when I went over to Jelka's bunk sometime later to tuck the bedclothes up around her shoulders, she said the exact same thing. "It'll be all right now," she said, and I bent down to pick up her figurine of Saint Brendan from where he had fallen on the floor.

The second half of the day went like this.

I was asleep, not in my bunk but on the main deck, which is why I didn't see all of it. I woke to a crash and to Matteo yelling, and when I came through to the rear chamber he was beating on the lower hatch leading to the escape trunk—through which, I came to understand, Jelka had just disappeared.

Escape trunks are a feature on most submarines and operate as a fail-safe in medium-depth waters, where the pressure of the ocean outside is intense but should nonetheless still be survivable if a person is able to exit in the correct diving gear. One climbs through an inner door, which is then sealed tightly, before engaging a switch that partially floods this closed-off section without needing to drown the entire craft. As the chamber floods, the air is simultaneously pressurized until it matches the pressure of the ocean against the outer doors, though a bubble of air remains at the top of the chamber to allow the person inside to continue to breathe. Once the pressure in the chamber is equal to the pressure outside, the outer doors can be opened and one can theoretically swim to safety. Of course, this is all predicated on the pressure outside not being such that the doors opening would result in one being instantly crushed.

I remember we tried the handwheel that opened the hatch and found it immovable. I remember we beat on the door, though I don't remember much of what we said. She had gone out, as Matteo would explain to me only later, while he was in the wash stall, she had been sitting at the table beforehand as if nothing was wrong. I remember the light above the hatch blinking on, to indicate the trunk was being flooded. I remember the clattering on of the internal mechanism that would cause the air in the chamber to change. I remember, too, the brief silence before the sound of the external doors opening, and then the rush of the water—miles and miles of it on top of our heads.

MIRI

I buy a length of surgical bandage and use it to bind up the side of Leah's face. The effect is semipiratical—the bandage sits at an inappropriately jaunty angle, covering up the place where her eye used to be. "Can you see?" I ask, and she nods, and that seems to be all there is to say.

She appears shaken but not exactly disturbed. She doesn't resist my hand at her cheek when I tip her head to check the bandage is lying straight. I put her back in the bath, because that is all I can think of to do with her, and bring her three tablespoons of salt dissolved in water.

"It'll be all right now," I hear her saying, in the brief time I'm out of the room, and I think of the very first days after her return, wiping the blood from her face in the bathroom: *be all right, be all right in a minute.*

For a while, I sit cross-legged on the bath mat with my back to the tub and watch the tail end of a movie about a talent competition. The crux of the plot appears to be that one girl is patently more deserving of a win than her competitors, one of whom seems willing to commit murder in order to secure the crown, and several times it occurs to me to turn and ask Leah if this is a movie we've seen together before. I am finding it hard to imagine that the Leah behind me is someone I could ever have simply watched movies with, someone I could really have wasted my evenings with doing nothing at all.

"Do you remember the pea and paneer?" she says, out of

nowhere, and when I don't immediately respond, she asks me the question again. "We used to order it," she says. "Mattar paneer and pilau, from the place that took your name and made you sit on a bench while they made it. And they'd always ask you if you wanted jalebi while you waited, even though it always seemed wrong, to eat the sweet thing first."

I don't turn around, though I know what she's talking about, know with a shock like a shoulder wrenched from its socket, like a stop and a sudden drop. I remember, the way that Leah also seems to be remembering, a time before we lived together, when I would stay at hers and we would walk to the Indian place on her corner, returning home with the greasy-hot bag swinging heavy between us and me always insisting we should have tried something different this time. I sit with my back to the bath and think about this, about the tight specific cold of the air when you leave the house late for hot food and the way that Leah always held the door for me before going inside herself. I think about this and I feel that it is suddenly *my* Leah again, my Leah in the bath behind me, and I am seized with a stark and immediate panic—a panic that I know I have allowed to wander on a leash for so long, mainly keeping it at a wary distance though always at least partially in view. That panic encloses me now, and I turn on my knees and lean up to kiss her in a way I haven't done in so long. She might move a hand up toward me, I'm not entirely sure. I half note the sensation of something damp against my cheek, of kissing her and then moving away and of trying to understand her face from this close after so many months of distance. "I remember that," I say, and I think she smiles at me, although everything is difficult under the bandages, truncated and harder to read. I take my clothes off and get into the bath with her, and though she seems to resist for a moment, she ultimately allows me to move, leaning up so I can get in behind her and resting back again after a moment to fit along my front.

"You'll be OK in here with me," she says and I don't ask her what she means by that. "I should have touched Jelka," she says. "Before, I mean. I should have tried when she reached for me."

Before, I mean.

It occurs to me that I know what happened to Jelka. Something of it, anyway. Juna looking at me frankly across the table: *I need to tell you that my sister is dead.* I try to think of something to say to Leah but nothing seems appropriate. Instead, I hold her and pretend her skin feels different—less temporary, less like something about to give way. It's terrible when you can't make something OK. As a hypochondriac, the typical response when I'm panicking is to acknowledge it will end. At some point, I will cease to be convinced that I have a brain tumor, or a stomach ulcer, or some degenerative condition of the nerves, and so at some point, the bad thing will end. When something bad is actually happening, it's easy to underreact, because a part of you is wired to assume it isn't real. When you stop underreacting, the horror is unique because it is, unfortunately, endless.

The neighbors play cooking shows at top volume for three days running and then abruptly switch over to something I am unable to identify but that appears to be the championship finals for some kind of niche American sport. Mist muscles up to the windows each morning, aggressive in its density, in the way it seems to gather up the light. Juna calls and asks if I want to talk to her and I tell her to give me more time. I call Carmen instead, but I have lost track of the days and she is having her eye operation. The woman who answers her phone asks if I want to call back for her voicemail and I don't bother to ask who it is I'm speaking to.

"I don't know why I expected you to read my mind," I say, when I call back to leave her a message. "I was just doing what I always do, assuming the world revolves around me."

I take my laptop to the sofa and open up the website for people whose loved ones have disappeared. I scroll through the message boards for several seconds, taking in the surprising number of new posts that have sprung up since I last logged on. *Problem is*, I read, *that ultimately you're really the one who has to kill them. Or not them but the idea of them—you have to make a choice to let it end.*

I sit there and think about Leah, the version of her I imagined before I met her, the gentle pressure when I pushed my lips in the cup of my own hand and pretended a kiss. I think about the way that we met, and then much later the way I assumed she was dead, after five months of radio silence—about how all you want to do in response to grief is talk about it but all everyone assumes you want to do is talk about anything else. I think about this, and about other things, and at some point I must fall asleep because I wake to a message from Sam and another from Toby: *Sam says she can't get hold of you and she's not sure whether or not to come around*. I go outside at about 3 A.M.—the kind of cold air that only seems to occur when you get a cab late or very early. I sit on the wall in front of our building and look across the road toward the grass. I imagine that I have wandered the wrong way through some door and found myself in an alternative, uninhabited version of things, but then a car streaks past playing music and everything is the same as it was.

When I come back inside, Leah is lying in the bath, the way I left her. She is faceup, entirely submerged—the pale wash of her remaining eye beneath the surface, the amniotic shiver of the water. The light in the bathroom is off, there is little illumination but for the orange glow from the streetlamps. I lean down over the water. It's hard to describe it—the way her chest seems to brim, a sensation of something teeming. As I look, I see that the skin across her ribs is pulling, clearing, growing transparent like a window wiped of mist. I see her ribs through her skin and then her lungs, expanding, retracting, the whole of her sheer in the water, translucent, transparent, and breathing easily, though—submerged as she is—she has no recourse to the air.

LEAH

Here are some things I find quite interesting:

1. The tides are the natural response of water to the gravitational pull of the moon and sun. Just as the moon will rise a certain number of minutes later every day, so high tide in most areas will be correspondingly later also. The difference between a high and low tide will be at its greatest at full or new moon, as this is the point at which Earth, the sun, and the moon are in line and most in concert, with gravity consequently exerting its greatest strength upon the sea.

2. There is no concrete theory as to the origin of the phrase "the seven seas," although it appears in various ancient Sumerian, Indian, and Roman texts, apparently as far back as 2300 BCE.

3. There are very possibly more historical artifacts in the ocean than in all of the world's museums, although more often than not I do wonder whether this is simply something people say, rather than a quantifiable fact.

4. Most of Earth's natural wonders owe their existence to bodies of water, in some way or other. Niagara Falls and its gorge, for example, date back to the Silurian period when a vast recess of the Arctic sea moved southward and deposited dolomite beds along what would

in time become the Niagara escarpment. Millions of
years later, water released from melting glaciers came
plunging over the edge of this escarpment, wearing
away at the shale beneath the dolomite and creating
what you would now recognize as the falls and its
gorge.

5. There is actually very little similarity between the
   chemical makeup of ocean water and river water, with
   the various compositional elements of each present
   in almost entirely different proportions. In rivers, for
   instance, you're likely to find something like four times
   as much calcium as chloride, whereas the exact opposite is the case for the sea. This difference is likely to
   be due to the number of ocean-dwelling animals that
   use calcium salts to build their shells and exoskeletons.
   Almost everything that lives in the ocean is also made
   up of the ocean, to some degree, rather like the way
   we inherit mitochondrial DNA from our mothers, and
   our cells likewise hang around in our mothers' bloodstreams for years after we're born.

These are all things that I know, but none of this is really
important. I used to think it was vital to know things, to feel
safe in the learning and recounting of facts. I used to think it
was possible to know enough to escape from the panic of *not*
knowing, but I realize now that you can never learn enough to
protect yourself, not really.

————

Matteo went down into the escape trunk once it had closed
again, when the drain valve had expelled the residual water

from the compartment. I didn't go down with him to look. When he came back, his face was odd, unpleasant. His hands were wet, as though he had run them across the still-damp interior of the compartment. I went to fetch a towel from the shower stall and dried his hands for him, and afterward I made coffee, and afterward he fell asleep. As he slept, I went out onto the main deck and looked toward the windows, willing something to appear and seeing nothing, the way I always saw nothing, and this briefly felt worse than the fact of what Jelka had done.

Later on, I found Saint Brendan of Clonfert in my bunk again and I held him up underneath the kitchen lights to look at him, his sculpted beard and the miniature galleon he cradled in one arm. I remembered Jelka leaning back to tell me a story—the trials of Saint Brendan, recounted over any number of nights on assignment years ago: *He meets Judas, one night during his voyaging. It's a subject you see a lot on stained-glass windows, actually, paintings, things like that. He travels for months on end, encountering demons, sea monsters, every kind of creature you can imagine, and then one night he comes upon a man chained to a pillar of rock, in the middle of the sea—just there, just there in the ocean like this great, tall fang rising from the waves, this thing that shouldn't be there, a man at the mercy of the elements. So Saint Brendan calls out to him and he learns that the man is Judas— Judas who gave Jesus up for dead, Judas the failed apostle—and Saint Brendan learns that Judas is there because the way in which the Lord chooses to show him mercy is to free him from his torments, to free him from hell on Sundays and Holy Days, and cast him adrift on the ocean, where he can at least feel the wind on his face. I always like that part of the story. Saint Brendan stays all night, until Judas's respite from his torments is over, and then he has to go on.*

At some point, the sound started up again, only this time, when it did, I heard the voice inside it. I mean by this, of course, that I heard the voice that Jelka had told us about, the voice I hadn't heard before, the voice she had claimed couldn't possibly be a ghost.

MIRI

I take to reminding Leah of things, inconsequential things: the way she always used to say *SMILE* aloud when someone photographed her, the way we used to argue quite often about something thoughtless one or the other of us had done in a dream. She is finding it hard to breathe outside the water now, so I'm not sure how much of this she hears. I think of dipping my head beneath the surface of the water to speak these recollections into her ear.

"Remember," I tell her, "the time that we met. In the bar where they were playing 'I've Got a Feeling.' And then you came up and spoke to me and the music changed to 'Horny,' and that's something I can't change now. Like, that's just the story. That's what happened. They played 'Horny' by Mousse T. in a bar full of straight people and that's the story of how we met."

I have taken to filling up glass ramekins with table salt and ferrying them into the bathroom, pouring the salt into the water and allowing it to dissolve. I'm not sure what prompted me to start doing this, although I'm fairly certain Leah appreciates it. On occasion, she will flick a hand up from the bathwater in a gesture I have decided to take as thanks.

Carmen calls me to tell me about her eye surgery. The after-effects are peculiar, she says, everything tinted a pale tangerine, the shades of figures that cannot be real rotating in the corners of her vision.

"They told me to expect this," she says, "so I'm not that worried. What's important is it all seems clearer than it was! Not perfect yet, but they said it should get better every day for a week. *Ad meliora*, et cetera, et cetera."

I feel winded by her happiness and don't know how to express this, ask her when she thinks she'll be up and about again.

"Anytime, really," she says. "I have these weird glasses I can wear to make sure I don't bump into things. They're different colored on each side, so it's a bit of a freak show, but I'm sure you'll recognize me."

But will you recognize me, I want to ask her, want to know how it is I will look in her new unencumbered vision, whether I will show up at all.

"Miri," Carmen is saying, and I'm unsure how long I've been silent, whether I have missed her saying something else. "You never told me anything. You told me she was delayed and then she came back and then it was *fine*. When you left that message, that was the first I'd heard of anything being wrong."

When they took my mother to the hospice, I spent a weekend alone at her house, packing things away. At the time I didn't really know Leah well enough to ask her to do this with me, though I remember wanting her there desperately and texting her almost without cease the entire weekend.

It was a strange time; I wasn't selling the house, only dust-sheeting it for some unspecified future point, and so the act of disposing of things was less cathartic than it might otherwise have been. This was not an endpoint so much as it was a suspension. I took out the rubbish, threw away anything perishable, locked up the valuables, and left everything else as

I'd found it: the living room dim, my mother's handkerchiefs in a pile on the dresser. There were Tupperware boxes in the fridge, steamed broccoli and an untouched chicken Kiev that my mother's nurse must have heated but then failed to convince her to eat. I thought about eating these myself but found the idea of it somehow distasteful and threw them away. Later on, I sat in my mother's chair near the windows and thought about the curious way she sometimes had of speaking to me more freely in bad weather, as though the rattle of sleet against the windowpanes might have served as a cover for her confidences. I used to think of it this way: with the rain, conversation. The atmosphere attempting openness and never quite achieving it, my mother returning to reticence before I ever had a chance to get a complete foothold. Often, when I would bring up later something she had said—her feelings on the divorce, her thoughts on something she had read and enjoyed—she would look at me with no small measure of confusion, so much so that I often thought that the very act of sharing was expunged from her mind as soon as it happened. *I don't think that sounds right*, she would often say, when I quoted herself back to her, and then carry on discussing something impersonal: the weather or the way a neighbor had of parking their car halfway across her drive and what she was going to do about it.

Below the windows, below the house, there runs the partially eroded charcoal road that leads down to the beach. Once down, you clamber across quartz-veined rocks that run down from the cliff face to reach the sand. The beach floods at high tide, leaving the tide pools alive with green crabs making for the relative safety of higher ground, jellyfish smashed to bits and uncoupled from themselves against the rocks. Sitting in my mother's chair that weekend, I watched the tide and did not consider making my way down. *I hope you're OK*, Leah messaged, and then sent me a picture of a cat she had seen on the pavement outside her building, a video of her making kissing noises at it and being ignored. *When your dad died*, I replied, *what did that feel like*, and then, *She's not dead, so this is a stupid thing to ask.*

LEAH

Matteo in his circle of torches on the main deck, blinking toward the windows. I came in from the rear chamber, wanting to ask how long he had let me sleep and aware it would be pointless to do so. He didn't acknowledge my presence, barely moving when I opened my mouth to speak.

"I could make you some coffee," I said, when several moments had passed and neither of us had said anything. Now that I think about it, I'm not at all sure how long it had been since I'd last spoken. Since Jelka, Matteo's and my cohabitation had receded to something empty, quiet for the most part. We moved around each other, gave each other a wide berth, as if still trying to factor Jelka into the space she had vacated. Sometimes, when I was in my bunk, I would slit one eye open and watch him without knowing why.

"You shouldn't keep sitting like that," I said when he didn't respond, gesturing to his crossed legs, the awkward hump of his back and neck. "Bad for your posture."

I don't know why I said this, really. All of us (*both* of us, I should say) had been cooped up so long that it seemed impossible to imagine our bodies looking the same as they had done on first immersion. Cramped living conditions, cramped bunks, air that was only rendered breathable by a trick of machinery. Sometimes I would catch my reflection in the windows and imagine I saw myself concertinaed by pressure, bent double, distorted out of any recognizable shape. This image would usually correct itself on second inspection, though not always. Lately, in fact, it was getting harder to see myself without the trace of something fundamentally unpleasant sketched over the top.

Matteo still wasn't responding to me, though he briefly leaned over as if to correct the alignment of one of the torches, then seemed to think better of it. I experienced an impulse to kick out at the torch nearest to me, sweeping a hole through the charm he imagined the circle cast, though I didn't do this.

"I should probably make something to eat," I tried again, when Matteo still chose to say nothing. I looked at the side of his face, the impassive expression, and felt briefly overwhelmed by rage. I'm not sure what this feeling was about, exactly, whether it was purely to do with Matteo ignoring me or rather a little of everything: the dark, the blank, the impossibility, the sheer pointlessness of everything we had so far been forced to endure. I looked toward the window, caught the bent, unhappy line of the thing that seemed to be my reflection and then closed my eyes quickly, thought about Miri instead. I wanted, as it suddenly occurred to me, to be hugged more desperately than I had possibly ever wanted it. I wanted to fit my head into the crook of her neck and feel her move her fingers through my hair.

"How will we ever explain this," I said, after another long moment. I meant Jelka, I suppose, but perhaps again I also meant a little of everything. I tried to picture explaining all that had happened to Miri, of taking out all the small observations I'd stored up for her and laying them down in a line, but when I did so the scene wouldn't run correctly. The imaginary me opened her mouth and produced only a strange, whaling ocean sound and the imaginary Miri couldn't be made to understand.

It was at this point that Matteo hung his head, his first movement that seemed to indicate that he had heard me speaking. He didn't say anything, though his shoulders moved a little, and after a long minute he moved to one side, gesturing for me to step inside his circle of torches. I came and sat beside him, our sides not quite touching, and we stayed like that for a long time before getting up again and going on as we had before. It was quiet—no sound and no voice within that sound, as though something were taking a breath. Time passed, I'm not sure how much of it, and for a long time nothing happened.

MIRI

The night is cold, white lights, a curve of moon like a finger crooked into a claw. On Tuesday, Leah started losing motion in one of her legs and now the other appears to be defeating her. The strange transparency of her skin is intermittent; I will look at her and see more than halfway through her and then nothing again, almost as normal. The opal sheen of her is recurrent but not consistent; her skin seems to flex between states, first skin and then abalone and then water and back again.

I understand that she needs more salt, but I'm running low and I don't want to leave her. I put my hand to her face, the place where her eye once was. I try to take her hand and experience the distinct impression that if I squeeze it, it will melt away into the water. There is a softness that wasn't there before, the sense of a semiporous membrane in place of what was once a solid scaffolding of muscle and skin.

It is after midnight when her breathing becomes bad enough that I am seized with a sudden mania for changing the bathwater. She has been lying in it for so long that there is a scum of dust over the surface and the salt is collecting across the upper planes of her body. I try to pull her from the water, although when I do so, her face is not as I remember it. She has been beneath the surface for days now and the shape of her expression without the distortion of water above her is something I am not prepared for, to the extent that I almost drop her back. It is hard to explain, the way I see her in the moment before she starts to gasp and protest at the air and her extraction from the water. The way her features sit in her face seems uncertain, as though they have been placed there only delicately and might at any point leak sideways, like ice melting off a curving surface. In the second before I drop her, I half expect her to sluice through my fingers. She goes down again—a sharp splash, water slopping forward over the edge of the bathtub and soaking my feet—drops back, her eye on me, her long-drenched bandage slipping sideways, and I realize as I watch her sink that I cannot keep her here.

I'm not sure what time it is when I call Juna, though she picks up right away. *I have a car*, she tells me after I've explained, *don't apologize, I barely sleep anymore as it is.* When I've hung up, I take every towel we have and wet them in the bathroom sink, one by one, then pour the rest of the table salt over each and allow it to soak into the fabric.

LEAH

I wasn't aware of the power returning, only that when it did we were on the main deck and that suddenly the light was not what it had been seconds previously. The overheads blinked back on, as casual as anything at all, along with the beams from the front of the craft, and at once we saw the darkness for what it was.

"Jesus Christ," said Matteo and then covered his mouth. "I mean—" He seemed frozen, looked toward the control panel without moving his neck, like a person being stalked by a jungle creature and desperate to avoid being seen. "Don't move," he said. "I don't know why. It might go off again. The power. It might notice we're still here."

I looked at him, noticed the tendons in his neck pulled taut, straining to keep his head from swiveling. "That's ridiculous, isn't it," he said, and then, "Jesus Christ," again.

"Fuck." My voice felt too big in my mouth, like I was trying to swallow something without first chewing sufficiently.

The lights along the control panel switches glowed a faint electric yellow, just the way they were supposed to do. Matteo's circle of torches, still upright as they were, seemed dimmed in the sudden brightness of the whole compartment. I could hear a faint whirring sound—the vibrations of a craft in order, of a working mechanism rattling suddenly to life.

Beside me, in the unaccustomed light, Matteo was sweating.

"This is insane," he said, and then, "we can go. If it works, we can surface. We could do it now."

He flicked his eyes, once again, toward the main panel; he remained frozen in place, as if convinced that a single move could trip a wire that would throw us back into darkness. "Jesus Christ," he said again, and I felt quite certain he was about to cry. "Are they *allowing* us to do this? Is this what those fucks want? Just to send us down and bring us back up again? Are they doing this or is something else doing this? What if it works?"

I remember I looked at him then and I thought, with a clarity I hadn't experienced in ages, that it wasn't supposed to be like this. I remember I looked at him then and I thought *Not yet*, just once, and then I looked toward the windows in the spill of the exterior lights. I have always felt there is something knowable about the sea, something within comprehension, and I knew that I couldn't allow the opposite to be true. We couldn't—and I felt this with a force like a taste, like copper washed up against the backs of my teeth—we couldn't go until I had *seen* it, until we had seen some vestige of what we had come down to see. *Not yet*, I thought to myself, once more and with a sort of ridiculous earnestness I can't defend, my body slack around me, everything suddenly superfluous but the desire to see what I needed to see.

"We will," I said then and thought about Miri once with a sharp stabbing pain, and Matteo looked at me.

"Buddy—"

"I promise you," and I was moving toward the main panel, my body little enough my own at this point that I barely felt aware of it. "I promise you we will before the power goes."

And Matteo was moving now, breaking out of his temporary freeze to come toward me. "Buddy, *please*," he said, and his hand moved across the outer edge of the border made by the torch circle to take hold of my arm. "We can *go*," he said, and I looked at his fingers, the blistered black skin that bubbled up toward the nails and the blank space toward the outermost point of the fist where nothing remained. I looked at his fingers and I said, "But you have to understand this, don't you? When you went ice fishing with your dad and you knew what was happening and you ignored it. When you told me you said you didn't want to ruin it, you didn't want to go just yet."

He held on to my arm, worked his mouth without producing a sound. Out of the silence there rose once again the voice I knew Jelka had been hearing, the voice I hadn't let her explain.

"I promise you," I said again. "We won't lose power. I promise. I just want to know," I said, without really meaning to say this part aloud, "I just want to know that it wasn't for nothing. I just want to know what's here."

He didn't release his grip on my arm, though he allowed me to move one step toward the panel and then another, his fingers loosening in the manner of someone dazed or briefly distracted, his face now turned toward the glass.

"I don't see anything different," he said, "even with the lights on. It doesn't look like anywhere at all."

I didn't follow his gaze, thought instead about the slow deep salt of the ocean and all I knew about it, thought instead about the lights of the craft and moving away from where we were into something new.

"It'll be OK," I said, and tugged my wrist gently away from his grasp. He appeared to let me go for a moment before blinking, grabbing once again for my arm and pulling it back as his eyes moved down from the windows and back to me.

"No—" he said, his voice falling downward from his mouth like something dropped. He tightened his grip on my arm, pulled me back with a force that should have been painful but left me strangely blank. "We're going to—" he started and paused again, his jaw working, raised his other hand in a gesture that might have meant anything.

"Are you going to slap me," I said, and he stopped, dropped my arm, and looked at his fingers, and I felt my unkindness in the twist of his mouth but found there was nothing I could say to make it better. "I don't—" I started, and then abandoned the thought, felt it slip from the upper drift of my mind to somewhere lower. *Sunken thoughts*, said a voice in my head that was not mine, and then I moved toward the main panel, ignoring the place where someone had smashed a segment of keyboard with a torch, preparing to wake up the main engine and pilot the craft across the ocean floor.

After this, Matteo did very little of anything, sat dumb as though unable to believe what I had said to him or what I was choosing to do. The craft responded to my controls with the ease of something that had never been out of commission, and I wondered with a semihysterical pinch of amusement whether we might simply have misunderstood the situation all along, taken a broken light for a craft that could not be moved. We slid through the water, the darkness opening out only into further darkness, the lights from the front of the craft and the sensors picking up a geography of irregular basalt, wide-open crags of rock that spoke to a broad crevasse—something deep and narrow into which we had fallen—and yet not one living thing. I'm not sure how long I moved us forward through this darkness, the strange emptiness opening up before us the farther we went. I remember now that I caught that smell again—

the burning flesh, the rendering of something too hot to keep its form—though I am not sure if that is something I really registered or something I superimposed over the memory at some later point.

Come on, I found myself thinking, as I had while staring out into the blank wide blackness of the window and longing only for some struggle of life. *Come on*, I found myself thinking, *give*.

And movement, then, as if in acknowledgment. At last, a movement in the dark.

MIRI

When Leah came back, they called me at an odd time to let me know—three o'clock, too late for lunch, my gaze trained on a patch of carpet that seemed slightly lighter than the space around it. I didn't realize at the time, but she had actually been back for two weeks when the Centre got in touch. *We have been operating a cautionary quarantine,* the woman on the phone explained to me, *as I'm sure you would expect.* I remember her tone as conversational yet curiously distant—distant in a literal sense, as though she was holding the phone away from her. The background noise was difficult to parse: a shuttling sound, a succession of jerkings and shudderings, as though someone was moving large pieces of furniture across the floor. *You're welcome to come and pick her up,* the woman on the phone informed me. I had to ask her for an address and then to wait while I fetched a pen.

I remember very little about that afternoon. I put on shoes and found they were the wrong ones for the weather but by that point I had already left the flat. I hailed a cab and did not ask about the price. The Centre was somewhere outside the city, a few minutes from the coast, but I couldn't tell you where exactly, or how big it was or even what it looked like. I remember only a car park, tumbleweeded through with crisp packets the way all car parks are, and a sickish lurch at the base of my ribs—perversely bridal with anticipation—and then Leah, suddenly present as though she had manifested, nothing on her but the clothes she wore, no bag, no nothing, as though they had bundled her out in a hurry. I remember this: the way she stood and looked at me, half raised her arms, and then dropped them, as though uncertain of her welcome, and the way I ran toward her anyway, the bright reality of her, and felt such wide white blinding love and relief that all other memories from that day disappeared.

———

Some twenty minutes after I call her, Juna is outside in a dark green Volvo; an ichthys decal in the back window above a sticker reading WOULD YOU FOLLOW JESUS THIS CLOSE? "My sister's car," she explains, when she catches me looking. "Don't have the energy to scrape the fuckers off."

She is wrapped up in a moleskin coat over what appear to be pajamas. She looks at me frankly—a stickiness of bed still clinging to her edges—and I find that I badly want to call Carmen or Sam or anyone at all who isn't the stranger in front of me now.

"So where are we going?" she asks in an even tone, as though the two of us are simply deciding where we might go for lunch. I tell her to follow me upstairs.

My neighbor's television can be heard from the communal stairwell, two reality stars from a show I don't remember the name of gossiping like ghosts in the walls. Climbing the stairs behind me, Juna raises her eyebrows. "Bit late for it," she says, and I appreciate this. It is because of this, I think, that I choose not to warn her, pushing open the bathroom door without first turning to say, *OK, so I know you won't believe this but.* Her reaction appears to justify this instinct—she appraises Leah in the bathtub, looks at me, eyes the towels I have piled, sopping wet, in the sink. "OK," she says, "so I guess we'll need water."

We fill several plastic bottles from the tap, take out the washing-up bowls I keep under the sink and fill them, too, mixing salt into each before ferrying them down to the Volvo. We place the washing-up bowls in the footwells behind the front seats and stack the bottles in the passenger seat before returning to the flat. "I can help you," Juna says, "if you want me to," but I ask her instead to go into my wardrobe and pack up whatever look like appropriate clothes for a trip. When she's out of the room, I pull Leah up out of the water as gently as I can, trying to ignore the rattling protest of her breath as she surfaces, the way her hand clenches down and then releases, the terrible softness of her body, like a plastic bag overfilled with water. I wrap her up in the saltwater-soaked towels, two around her torso and another at her legs, mermaiding her thighs together, twisting two damp cloths around her wrists where the pulse beats fast and fluid. I leave her face until last, lift her up and look at her, at the traces of a person I still recognize, and then Juna calls from the other room and I think to myself *OK* and then I take the white flannel from the edge of the sink and I press it over her face.

I feel very little as I do this. I think *I am going to take care of you* and then I think about Leah, Saturday mornings, going through our electric bill or our gas or water bill because she knew it was something I hated to do, and then I think nothing at all.

In the car, I stretch her out across the backseat, hold her head in my lap, and listen to the shiver of her breathing through the salt-wet flannel. Every so often, I will take this flannel away from her, dip it in one of the basins of water at my feet, and return it to her face again. I give Juna directions and imagine our upstairs neighbors waking up in the morning somehow knowing that their television now only plays to an absence below. The night is dark and Juna drives us into it and I feel vaguely doomed, vaguely certain of an ending I can't see.

LEAH

Miri said this to me once: Every horror movie ends the way you know it will. If you're watching a movie about werewolves, you can be almost certain your hero will become one by the end. If you're watching a movie about vampires, same thing. Ghosts, too, I think, if the hero wasn't already a ghost to begin with. I thought about this a little, at the end of things. I pressed my hands into the glass and knew the thing I'd always known: that we were in the ocean and that we couldn't be alone.

We had come to what appeared to be a kind of drop, the crevasse into which we had fallen widening out for some meters before stopping sharply at what, on sight, resembled a valley in the ocean floor. On taking a read from the sensors, however, I saw that what appeared to be a gentle dip was in fact a great break, a chasm in the ground beneath us like something shattered or pulled apart—vast staggers of basalt scattering downward into a chasm that appeared to fall some hundred feet beneath the point at which we currently sat. For several moments I tried to make sense of this, the idea that there could be somewhere deeper still beneath us, the idea of what the blackness of this new drop might enclose. But then, of course, I stopped trying, stopped reading from the sensors or expecting to make sense of anything at all.

During all this, you must understand, I had been aware and not aware of the burning smell that had dogged so much of our time below the water, aware yet not aware of the sound that had curled around our craft for so long, the sound we had heard so often and the voice inside that sound. You have to understand this, understand the way I sensed these things getting closer—the smell and the sound—or rather our growing closer to them, and yet did not put together an explanation for any of this. You have to understand that there was no way for me to know, no way for me to predict what I was doing, because how could I, really. How could I know something that simply could not be the case.

I remember I saw it—the eye, and then the face beyond the eye, the way it rose up from the chasm below us and kept rising, the way it filled the windows, filled my field of vision, seemed to fill the whole ocean by itself. I don't know how to tell you this, really. I remember thinking of the octopus I had cared for, years ago at the aquarium, I remember thinking of the creatures I had seen in tide pools with my father as a child, the strange spiny things that raced for the water when the tide began to wane. I remember thinking that the first things had come from the water, which didn't account for the things that had chosen to stay behind. I remember thinking all of this and then thinking that it wouldn't help me and then thinking that the creature before us was still rising, that it now stretched up toward us, the eye rearing toward our ship. Somewhere beside me, Matteo might have made a sound, might have spoken to me, I couldn't tell you now. I thought about Jelka telling me the thing she was hearing simply couldn't be a ghost. I thought about this, and I tried to listen to what it was I was hearing, what this creature was saying to me—really tried to listen, to separate the fact of the voice from the words themselves. I remember that, but I don't remember whether I understood anything, whether the words shaped themselves into anything like sense down there, in the place we shouldn't have fallen to. I remember only the vastness of the creature rising up before us and a sudden certainty that it had been here all along.

The eye moved in, still closer, and somewhere beside me I felt Matteo moving back. Myself, I did not feel so much unable to move as lacking the energy to do so. I looked into that eye, now filling the entire view of the windows, and I felt, with an exhaustion that sat down inside me as though unable to support its own weight, that there would never be any way of knowing whether we had come here intentionally, whether we had been pulled down or pushed. I felt all this and then I passed my hand over the panel—the small etched image of an eye, which was not the Centre's logo, which did not appear to stand for anything at all—and reached for the leather logbook and pen, which we kept beneath the central console, thus far untouched. I pulled these out and, without pausing to consider what I was doing, I wrote my name on the first page of the logbook and pressed it to the window, so that the creature could see.

MIRI

Sometimes, I imagine my mother and Leah meeting, though this is not a thing that ever actually happened. In the fantasy, if fantasy is quite the word, this typically takes place at my mother's house by the sea, and perhaps my mother has never been ill, or perhaps she has but I haven't failed her, I have chosen to take better care of her and this has saved her, in whatever impossible way. Most of the time, what happens is that she and Leah get along so well that they start having little jokes that exclude me and I enjoy this enormously. Some of the time, Leah takes my mother down to the beach below the house and tells her something she has told me many times before: we think of the place we live as important, but that a far greater percentage of the world is made up of the ocean and that most of the creatures that live on the planet live there. In this dream, if dream is quite the word, my mother tells her that that's a terribly pretentious thing to say and this makes Leah laugh, which is what makes my mother like her.

———

We arrive in the early morning—white mist on the ground like a trip wire, my mother's house as yet untouched by the first of the light. Juna has driven at what seems to me a mad pace for a route she is unfamiliar with, but I can't deny that when we round the elm grove that covers the headland and come down into the final stretch of road, I feel a sort of wild relief I have really not expected and I lean forward to tell her so.

"Nothing easier," she says, waving a hand. "Do you think I can park just anywhere?"

At this point I haven't been to the house in several years, have expressed the intention of selling it on more than one occasion and then failed to follow through. Selling it, in some way, seemed like the last thing, and so instead I gutted it of its useful attributes, stole its furniture, pulled its teeth, and left it standing as it was. Once inside, the main rooms carry a particular chill of disuse, blank spaces on the walls stained darker colors by the missing frames and photographs. In the main room, I pull the dust sheets from the sofas and briefly feel my mother at my elbow, though when I turn, her chair is empty. In the doorway, Juna clears her throat and I turn, find her leaning there with a shadow in the passage behind her, which, again, I take to be my mother, though in truth it is only the shape of Juna's coat, which she has removed and hung from a hook on the door.

"We should get her out of the car," I say, and she nods at me.

"And then I need a cup of tea."

"I can turn the water on at the mains, but I'm not sure where you're going to find a tea bag."

We get Leah in, somehow, move her up to my mother's bathroom, where I pour the salt water into the bath from the bottles we have brought before filling it the rest of the way from the taps. I unwrap her from her towels as gently as I can and maneuver her into the water, her hair like a halo and her bandage slipping down to reveal the wide dark space where her eye should be. I kneel down by the side of the bath and ask her to forgive me for moving her, for the car journey she had been in no position to approve. "It just seemed like the best thing," I say to her, noticing as I do so that the remains of her face are weeping sideways in the water, becoming something less like flesh and more like liquid. "It just seemed like something I had to do."

When I was younger, I think some glib or cavalier part of me always believed that there was no such thing as heartache—that it was simply a case of things getting in past the rib cage and finding there was no way out. I know now, of course, that this was a stupid thing to think, insofar as most things we believe will turn out to be ridiculous in the end.

The day is cold, too long because we started early, washed curiously blank by the rain that comes in off the sea and lasts well into the afternoon. For the most part, I stay in the bathroom with Leah, though at irregular intervals, Juna comes in offering cups of tea, a sleeve of Penguin biscuits, explaining that she took the car back up across the tops and stopped to buy supplies at a petrol station she had noticed on the way in. At some point, I suppose at lunchtime, she tells me she thinks I ought to come downstairs and eat something, and when I refuse, she comes and sits with me in the corridor outside the bathroom with a plastic plate of sandwiches and the door ajar, and tells me some of what she knows.

She tells me that when the craft surfaced, only Leah and one other crew member were aboard, that she isn't sure of the other crew member's name or condition.

"I have to assume the same happened to them as Leah," she says, "or is happening to them. Whoever they were. Or maybe I don't. Maybe they quarantined like Leah and went home just fine. Maybe they're fine now. I don't know how we find out." *I remember his name*, I think of telling her, *I remember Leah worked with him before.*

She tells me that the Centre informed her via letter of her sister's accidental death during the course of the dive and explained that, as was regulation, the body had been expelled from the craft while still submerged. She had not been encouraged, she said, to come down to the Centre, but did so anyway after several unhelpful phone calls, as she believed they might be in possession of various of her sister's effects. She tells me, only as an aside, that during the long absence of the dive, she had grown increasingly convinced that someone with information was trying to call her on the phone. "You said it happened to you," she says, "which is why I mention it. Sometimes I thought it was someone from the Centre, too, someone trying to warn me and losing their nerve. Other times I imagine it was all just a practical joke. The whole thing can feel like a joke to me now, a little, so I'm not sure I'd even be surprised." On arriving at the Centre, she had been told that Leah and the other crew member were both in quarantine and that any personal belongings would be subject to the same restrictions. She tells me, calmly enough, that an altercation followed. This is how she describes it, too: "There was an altercation. I mean, you have to understand, my sister's dead and here's some bitch at what amounts to a front desk at this creepy place I've never visited before telling me I can't have, what, her shoes? Her underwear? These weird fucking people—I remember Jelka when she first got the job, she just kept saying, *These people are weird*. So I start arguing, obviously, I tell them I'm going to go to the newspapers, or get a lawyer, that all of this sounds wrong to me, that they never told us what was happening when they went down and didn't come up. I say all kinds of crazy shit, that I think they hired them under false pretenses—that my sister and the rest didn't know what it was they were getting into, that it was all a sham, and on and on like that—until eventually some other guy comes out and I tell him no I don't want a fucking supervisor I want whoever is the most senior person at this place. And then finally this guy appears, this guy who's wearing a fucking sports coat, mind you, like a sports coat and *jeans*, and he tells me hey, my name is *whatever*—see, I don't even remember his name—and he tells me that of course he wants to help."

She tells me that after this other man appeared (Leah, in the back of my mind, jokingly referring to *The Boss* at the going-away party), everything was easy, that they gave her sister's effects to her, as though there had never been an issue, that he even passed her a personal number and told her to call him if there was anything else he could do. "It was weird," she says, "this weird loopy little attitude he had, like it was all fine, like he could make it fine. I didn't think to try the number until a few weeks afterward, but of course when I rang it there was just a message saying the line was no longer in service. It was meant to be a research trip, you know. Just observing, taking notes. I don't know what it really was, but I've been trying to find out."

She sits beside me in silence for a while after this, still—as it only occurs to me now—in last night's pajamas, her skin without makeup the consistency of something clawed with a fork. I say nothing, only glancing at my sandwich and thinking, in a dull sort of way, that this should all be more interesting to me than it is. "I think," Juna says, after a pause, "that the thing about losing someone isn't the loss but the absence of afterward. D'you know what I mean? The endlessness of that." She looks sideways at me and sniffs. "My friends were sad, people who knew my sister were sad, but everyone moves on after a month. It's all they can manage. It doesn't mean they weren't sad, just that things keep going or something, I don't know." She rolls her shoulder, shakes her head. "It's hard when you look up and realize that everyone's moved off and left you in that place by yourself. Like they've all gone on and you're there still, holding on to this person you're supposed to let go of. *Let go of them in the water* is something I read once. Seems a bit of a joke in the circumstances, but still. Something about how living means relinquishing the dead and letting them drop down or fall or sink. Letting go of them in the water, you know."

I look at her and I feel a collection of curious things, none of which feel quite correct for the circumstances. I feel the coolness I always feel toward strangers, the gentle yawn of distance I still can't help but preserve, even despite her sharing all of this with me. I feel, too, the blank exhaustion of everything, the fact that I should not be out here but in the bathroom with Leah, the fact that I need to message Carmen and tell her I hope her eyes are doing better, the fact that I need to call Sam and apologize for dropping off the face of the earth. I lean my head back against the wall for a second and then roll it sideways until it is resting on Juna's shoulder. She allows me to do this, hunches up a little to prevent me stretching my neck, and for a moment I am able to banish my other thoughts and feel only what I ought to feel, which is grateful.

———

Here are some things I didn't have space for:
    Putting on "Alone" by Heart and miming the lyrics in Leah's face until she started laughing.

    Leah's long hands and her yellow hair and the werewolf quality to her eyebrows. The way she walked around the flat in shorts and a sports bra and told me off for staring. The way she kissed me and then apologized for biting.

    The time Leah told me that making me laugh was always an achievement because my face was so typically set against it.

    The way I was often bored and Leah never was.

    Talking with Leah on early dates about the panic of doing what everyone else was doing and then feeling like a dick about it.

    The way Leah was kind by nature, where I always seemed to have to struggle. The way she tipped my face toward hers and told me otherwise—*You're the kindest person I know, and I know six or seven people.*

———

So here's what happens, obviously.
    Morning again—a rain that persists at first, grows full and hammering in its insistence and then passes away without

warning, a white sky, the windows filled with sharp corners of sunlight. I had not intended to take Leah down to the water, but when I wake beside the bath, having apparently fallen asleep with my cheek against the lip of the tub, I catch the direction of her remaining eye beneath the surface, the way it turns toward the window, and I think, *Well, yes.*

I soak the towels again, wrap her up as before, and maneuver her down the stairs. I find Juna lying awake on one of my mother's sofas, still in pajamas and with one arm pillowed behind her head. She doesn't ask me where I'm going or whether she needs me to come with her, only nods her head toward the moleskin coat still hanging from the hook on the door and tells me there is something in the pocket she'd like me to have. "Later on," she says, "if you like. It was in with Jelka's things when they gave them to me but it's actually Leah's, something she wrote—pages and pages. I brought it to give to you the first time we met, but it didn't seem like you'd want to take it. It's how I knew to come and find you. Not," she adds, with the strange sort of smile I am just about getting used to, "that you ever asked."

It is not difficult getting Leah down to the water. You might imagine it would be, but by this point the lightness in her body adds little to the weight of the towels that I've used to bundle her up. I take her up into my arms and carry her out toward the smuggler's path: a narrow track cut down into the cliffside that rears around my mother's house. Protected from the worst of the wind by a high tangle of gorse, which grows up like a wall along its sea-facing side, the path is more tunnel than lane, enclosed by an overarching shrubbery. I focus on my feet, on the tight nestle of Leah in my arms, and I think about nothing very much besides the rattle of her breathing and the fact that I have not heard her voice in something like two weeks. The path winds farther down the cliffside and along for several minutes before turning suddenly inland, rising up steeply and then evening out as we emerge at last onto a flat and grassy overhang, which juts out above a narrow inlet some feet below. Pausing to catch my breath, I glance down over the edge, where a system of caves reveals itself, flooded by waves in the waning tide. One fork of the path we are standing on splits off and straggles downward—a precarious but viable route down to the beach.

"Smugglers used to stow rum in those caves," I say now, my voice conversational, something I barely recognize. "Did I ever tell you that? Rum, brandy, tea leaves, whatever they could get. They could moor here in good weather without being seen. Town's too far inland for anyone to have heard them or seen them coming in. See those rocks just before the base?" I nod my head in the direction of the water, look down at Leah as though expecting her to respond. "You could throw a rope around just about any one of them, no problem at all. Tide's never completely out here—this part of the headland juts out so far—but it's dry toward the backs of the caves most of the time, so it was the perfect place to store things you didn't want to be found. Sometimes they'd even sleep there. Those caves go pretty far back but they certainly don't get roomier the farther in you get. I knew a boy at school who got stuck there once for almost a day and a half. Just mucking about, you know. I think he did it on a dare. Eventually the coastguard had to come and fish him out. We got to watch the whole thing from the house, my mother and me. I don't think I ever told you that. I don't know why I didn't."

The beach is just over the next rise, the sand curving like a bite taken out of the coastline, a mile at least toward a rocky outcrop that seems to mark its natural end. The sea reels outward, the tide some distance off and still retreating, revealing an extra inch of sand with every heave.

It is early still, deserted but for us, and I know what I am doing now.

I take her down toward the water, feet sinking in wet sand—lugworm tunnels, oarweed stretching up the beach like clambering hands. The water, when it penetrates my shoes, is freezing, the tight cold climbing sharply up my ankles, but I continue outward, down into the water until the tide is at my calves and then my knees. I keep Leah high in my arms, move farther, press my feet into the sand when the water is at chest height, kick my legs and push us farther, hold her in as closely as I can. The waves are gentle here, an easing surge of early morning. I no longer have much purchase on the sand, one leg tangled up with seaweed, mouth filling once with water, then again. I have never been a very good swimmer, even after Leah's lessons, and it is this thought, this memory that makes me grasp her tighter, pulling her into me from where my arms have slackened with the cold. A desperate squeeze inside my heart. My Leah—the way she held me around the waist at the lido and told me to kick, told me that she would buoy me along. My Leah.

But I can see it happening already, look down at her in my arms as the towels fall away, weighed down by the water that has saturated each in turn and left them too heavy to cling. Passingly, I think that this might always have been inevitable, that perhaps she had always known it but had wanted to hold on for me, for as long as she could. I can see it now, the way her chest begins to frill, the upward swell and tremor of the skin that registers its natural habitat, growing first translucent, then entirely clear. I can feel, as well, the way the body I am holding is becoming less a body, the way she slides between my fingers—first my Leah, then the water, first my Leah's arms, her chest, her rib cage, then the water they are struggling toward. I think of nothing, then I think about the sea lung, the day on the beach with Leah where the ice sat on the water and the air around us seemed about to take some other form. This alchemist sea, changing something into something else. I think of this and I look at her face, the remains of her face, my Leah. She is looking at me—this now, the last of her—and she is still looking at me when I move my arms to release her, when she melts between my hands and into water, twisting down into the rolling tide.

What persists after this is only air and water and me between them, not quite either and with one foot straining for the sand.

LEAH

We surfaced, of course. This is something to remember—
that we turned toward the panel after who knows how many
hours spent staring into that eye and told the craft to take us
upward. That we grasped each other's hands, Matteo and I,
and begged a being neither of us believed in to allow us to
surface. I don't remember much about the rest. I know the
creature did not stop us, though its eye held a strange, anticipatory expression as we receded, if "expression" is the word I
want. I know, too, that Matteo held on to Jelka's rosary beads
as we rocketed upward, as we moved up from darkness into
further dark, the light so many miles above our heads. I know
all this, and I know that as my head cleared, finally, of everything, sunken thoughts receding with the thing that we had
left below, I thought to myself *Miri Miri Miri* and I waited for
the ocean to end.

A NOTE ON THE TEXT

In case you haven't guessed, I am not a marine biologist. However, in my willful imitation of one, I've been lucky to rely on some incredible books and articles, particularly the following:

The Sea Around Us—Rachel Carson (Staples Press)
The Soul of an Octopus—Sy Montgomery (Atria Books)
"Thirty-six Thousand Feet Under the Sea"—Ben Taub
 (*The New Yorker*)
"Her Deepness"—Wallace White (*The New Yorker*)

I'm also highly indebted to Neal Agarwal's Deep Sea resource: neal.fun/deep-sea.

In addition to this, a couple of nonmarine texts were crucial to shaping the preoccupations that in turn shaped this book. I am grateful in particular to Annie Proulx's *The Shipping News* (4th Estate), for fostering a decade-long obsession with sea lungs, and Claire Cronin's *Blue Light of the Screen* (Repeater Books), for making me think about the intersection between ghosts and demons in a new and different way.

ACKNOWLEDGMENTS

To Ansa Khan Khattak and Caroline Bleeke. Most people are lucky to have one editor, so for this book to have two such dedicated champions feels like a wild and undeserved luxury.

To Kish Widyaratna, for seeing this book on its way with such grace and generosity.

To Sam Copeland, with thanks for infinite patience and humor.

To Alice Dewing and Katie Bowden: not only the best but also the coolest.

To Sydney Jeon, Marissa Constantinou, Nicholas Blake, Katie Haines, and everyone else who played a part in getting this book off the ground.

To Eleanor Harris, Cordelia and Ed Harper-Masters, Jess and Ash Burton, Pete Quigley and Amanda Williams, Lucy Baraona, Katie Clark, Daisy Mortimer, Sellisha Lockyer, Kerry Upham, Sophie Jagger, Hannah Leach, Emma Waring, Gabriella Shimeld-Fenn, Beans Webster and Jess O'Sullivan, Lindsay Smith, Greg Barrett, Eliza Clark and George Royle, Alison Rumfitt, Peter Armfield and Sarah Crowden, Elizabeth Macneal, Mikaella Clements and Onjuli Datta, Pete Scalpello, Alice Slater, Kirsty Logan, Heather Parry, Rosalind Jana and Marlena Valles, Nina Harvey-Brewin, and, of course, Louise Bower—for watching movies, for reading drafts, for making drinks, for sending messages, for all of that.

To Martha Perotto-Wills and Avery Curran, beloved coterie.

To Isobel Woodger and Sarvat Hasin, my forever girls.

To Tiggy, who did nothing.

To Mum, Dad, Nick, and Emily, with absolutely all of my love.

And to Rosalie—the only person I could be trapped with for over a year and still want more of everything.

This book is offered in memory of Michael Waring, a fellow shark lover and someone I wish I could have known better.

ABOUT THE AUTHOR

Julia Armfield is the author of the story collection *salt slow* and the novel *Our Wives Under the Sea*. Her work has been published in *Granta*, *The White Review*, Best British Short Stories 2019 and 2021, *Lighthouse*, and various other publications. She is the winner of the White Review Short Story Prize and a Pushcart Prize, and she was short-listed for the Sunday Times Young Writer of the Year Award in 2019. She lives and works in London.